irish girl

stories

Previous Winners of the Katherine Anne Porter Prize
in Short Fiction
Laura Kopchick, series editor

The Stuntman's Daughter by Alice Blanchard
Rick DeMarinis, Judge

Here Comes the Roar by Dave Shaw
Marly Swick, Judge

Let's Do by Rebecca Meacham
Jonis Agee, Judge

What Are You Afraid Of? by Michael Hyde
Sharon Oard Warner, Judge

Body Language by Kelly Magee
Dan Chaon, Judge

Wonderful Girl by Aimee La Brie
Bill Roorbach, Judge

Last Known Position by James Mathews
Tom Franklin, Judge

irish girl

stories

by tim johnston

University of North Texas Press
Denton, Texas

10 9 8 7 6 5 4 3 2 1

Permissions:
University of North Texas Press
1155 Union Circle #311336
Denton, Texas 76203-5017

∞The paper used in this book meets the minimum requirements of the American National
Standard for Permanence of Paper for Printed Library Materials, z39.48.1984. Binding
materials have been chosen for durability.

Library of Congress Cataloging-in-Publication Data

Johnston, Tim, 1962–
  Irish girl / by Tim Johnston.—1st ed.
    p. cm.— (Katherine Anne Porter Prize in Short Fiction series ; no. 8)
  2009 winner, Katherine Anne Porter Prize in Short Fiction.
  ISBN 978-1-57441-271-0 (pbk. : alk. paper)
  1. Fathers and sons—Fiction. I. Title. II. Series: Katherine Anne Porter Prize in Short
Fiction series ; no. 8.

  PS3610.O395I75 2009
  813'.6—dc22
                              2009025771

Irish Girl is Number 8 in the Katherine Anne Porter Prize in Short Fiction Series

Text design by Carol Sawyer/Rose Design

This book is for my brothers, Tad, Tyler, & Harris
& my sister, Tricia

Contents

Acknowledgments

Some of the stories in this collection have appeared elsewhere, in slightly different form: "Jumping Man" in *Best Life Magazine*; "Lucky Gorseman" in *Colorado Review*; "Water" at GivalPress. com; "Dirt Men" in *New Letters*; and "Irish Girl" in *DoubleTake Magazine*, the 2003 *O. Henry Prize Stories*, and *Children Playing Before a Statue of Hercules*. Grateful acknowledgment is made to these publications and their editors.

In addition, I wish to thank Marianne Merola and Joanne Brownstein for their hard work on behalf of these stories, Janet Peery who chose this collection for the Katherine Anne Porter Prize, Karen DeVinney who improved it for press, and The Mac-Dowell Colony for two very good months in the fall of 2008.

Dirt Men

It's old Jimmy Day who finds it, digging away on a tract of greasy earth that two days ago was an auto salvage lot. (Where those dripping wrecks ended up we don't ask: our focus has been on leveling the land so that pavement can get in there and lid the whole toxic stretch with two feet of concrete, pronto.) I was about twenty yards away on my skidloader, pushing around a green goulash of mud and batteries and hubcaps, looking right at Jimmy when he did something you almost never see Jimmy do: he stopped digging. His bucket came up, but instead of swinging over to the dump truck it halted, and hung there, bobbing, then folded up on itself like a stork leg so Jimmy could get a better look at what was inside, and—Holy Jesus: An arm. A human arm, jutting from the teeth. The arm so stark, and clean, and well-formed, it was impossible to think it was real.

Jimmy climbs down and walks his jerky, haywire walk over to it, and I join him there. The hand at the end of the arm is open, the fingers splayed, like, Whoa, stay back.

"Son of a bitch, Jimmy," Garth Koepke calls, grunting down from his dump truck, "what'd you do?"

"I ain't done nothin'," Jimmy says with a body-twitch. "I been just diggin'."

"Mother. Of. Christ," says Don Sherman around a wad of chaw, joining us. "Jesus, Rain Man." Ten years ago Don Sherman and I made it through four years of high school without word one to each other, and now he's foreman of me and all these old boys twice our age. He calls Jimmy *Rain Man* because of Jimmy's way with a backhoe, a machine that is like a twelve-ton drum kit, all pedals and levers, but he's the only one; Jimmy and his quirks are too old for a new nickname, especially one coined by Don Sherman.

More dirt men come round for a look. Up close we can see the grime in the creases of the palm and under the nails, which are long like a woman's and painted some dark shade. The air is a bad mix of diesel and river and spoilage, and the bluebottles have come. Seeing just the arm, and a jut of scapula, and a sprig of dirty hair, we all have the same queasy thought, but no one moves: the last gouge marks from Jimmy's bucket—the deep, vertical grooves from the teeth—hold us back.

"Jimmy," Don Sherman says at last. "Go on and see if you— you know. Got the whole deal."

Jimmy's right arm shoots spasmodically out, up, then down on top of his Cubs cap. "Well, Don. I don't . . . I don't—"

"Relax, Jimmy," Garth Koepke says with a hard glance at Don Sherman. "I'll go." He makes his way to the edge of the hole and, lowering to one knee, strikes a kind of pose, as if he is all at once a man burdened by deep thoughts.

"Well?" says Don Sherman.

Garth keeps looking, unmoving, pondering—until at last he stands and comes slowly back.

"Came out clean," he says, and everyone breathes again. Except the girl, inside Jimmy's bucket. All of her in there, tucked into the same shape, the same egg of earth, in which she'd been buried—just the arm extending, the hand open, trying to reach something, someone. No one speaks, and in the silence a few words, a sentence fragment, passes before my eyes like a banner behind a ghost plane:

far off as a star and just as small

I recognize it. I know its author. My student. My brilliant, tiny accuser.

———∞∞———

If Garth Koepke or Jimmy Day or any of the dirt men are Veterans of Foreign Wars, they have never made a point of it in my presence. Never hiked up sleeves to show tattoos or bullet holes. Never talked of the Nam, or Baghdad. But they are veterans of filing into the VFW Lounge on a hot July afternoon, sauntering in and forming such quick, unspoken subsets that right away I know I'm sitting with Jimmy Day: he may be Mozart on the backhoe but on the ground he's still a spaz, and I may be the only son of Buddy Knudson, one-time co-owner of Schotz & Knudson Excavating Co., but I am still that kid, that moody little jag-off they remember from ten years ago—Buddy Jr.

Junior, to the dirt men, then and now.

What compels Garth Koepke to join me and Jimmy is anybody's guess, maybe nothing more than the same stripe of antagonism that used to inspire in me such daydreams as I drove my little skidloader through the dirty summers: yonder came fat Garth, all aflame from his burning rig; here was his fat outline in the dirt, pancaked by a roller; there went his head, sailing like a teed-up golfball with one swing of Jimmy's bucket . . .

He takes a chair across from me with his fat man's huff, though he is easily half the size he used to be—hardly recognizable as the man I once hated so purely. And then he speaks:

"I don't know if you know this about Jimmy, Junior, but them retard legs a his is both hollow. He can drink you, me, and the Queen a England under this table."

I glance at Jimmy, to read his reaction, but he wears that Cubs cap like a roof and won't look up. "I do enjoy the beer," he says from under there.

Garth gazes dully at me, then past me, and squints, and says: "Goddam, Eddie, turn that up," and all the dirt men turn to look. It's the Biopark, up on an old Zenith behind the bar—an aerial view that momentarily telescopes toward earth, then snaps up again like a bungee jumper. The target is the stilled yellow hulk of Jimmy's backhoe, the bucket wrapped in blue tarp. Cops and other miniatures mill around doing important work. The bartender, Eddie, abandons the prying of bottlecaps to reach and jiggle a knob—an actual knob—until a female voice squawks out, "THAT'S RIGHT, JOHN AND LISA, THE LOCATION DOESN'T APPEAR TO BE THE BIOPARK ITSELF BUT SOMEWHAT, UM, SOUTH OF THAT. POSSIBLY THE SITE OF A HOTEL, OR A RESTAURANT . . ."

"It's a parking lot, sweetheart," says one of the dirt men.

They watch the coverage glumly, the dirt men, wondering if they'll have jobs come Monday. And maybe they won't. The Biopark Project, a head-scratcher from the beginning—twenty acres of simulated rainforest, indoors, in Iowa—has been taking a beating in the press, and nobody knows when the plug might get pulled, or what little thing might pull it.

We watch, and the old bartender with his eye patch makes the rounds, setting down beers with a repetitive thunk that sends each man into the same silent, automated motion of lifting, swigging, and setting the bottle down again, one after the other like men of some order, or church. Two months ago I was living in Colorado, riding my mountain bike, teaching my students, writing my book. I can tell myself these things but I can't quite believe them; all of that was a dream. Or else this is. I take my swig.

A lighter flares and I turn to see Garth lighting up. Others are smoking, there's the tack of nicotine everywhere. He jabs the pack at me and I decline.

"Been a while since I saw anybody light up indoors," I say, and he bares a dog's mouth of yellow teeth. "There is something wrong," he says, "something is off at the heart of things when a man can't light up where he pleases. Might as well tell him he can't say what he thinks, nor pledge allegiance, hey? Nor own a goddam pea-shooter except in the designated goddam areas." He glares at me like I have had something to do with these things. Like I've been away these ten years enacting legislation.

"I don't mind it," I say. "It reminds me of Buddy Senior."

"Buddy was a good man," Jimmy says.

Garth grunts and looks away.

"But he got the cancer anyway, didn't he, Junior Buddy."

"Christ, Jimmy," Garth says.

"Yes he did," I say. "He got it anyway."

Garth turns his squint on me again, through a cobra of smoke. "He went fast, hey Junior?"

Throughout the bar are photographs of soldiers: entire companies lined up like high school football squads. Smaller units arm-in-arm in front of tanks and helicopters. If the men are not trying to look like killers they are grinning like boys, but the effect from frame to frame is the same: *We died like this, young and far from home, in a manner you can't imagine.*

"About a week, altogether," I say. "I had to finish some things at school . . . final exams. I was on the plane when he passed." Garth knows this already—everybody knows it—yet I can't help explaining. As if Buddy Sr. himself were listening.

I take a swig with my eyes on the ceiling fan. Four sooty blades generating just enough turbulence to keep the flystrips corkscrewing.

"Well," Garth says, looking away. "Least you tried."

———— ∞ ————

Eddie jiggles the knob again in time for us to hear a reporter ask the Police Chief if there's any connection between the Biopark body and a middle-school science teacher who went missing two weeks ago. The Police Chief pats his moustache like it's a glue-on and says they are certainly looking into that possibility. Says, "It's unfortunate all those cars got hauled away. There might've been some evidence in there. At the same time, this person's remains might never have been recovered otherwise . . . so it's kind of a paradox for us."

"That's a strange word," I say. "Recovered. Shouldn't it be *un*covered?"

Garth pokes a pinky into his mouth to dig something from his teeth. "You're pissed, Junior."

"Junior Buddy enjoys the beer," Jimmy says. He raises his bottle in a strangely steady salute.

"Naw," I say.

"It's all right," Garth says.

Fuck you, old man.

Newscopter Nine is filming the portage of a large white bag across the dig site. It takes a surprising number of people to carry the bag—she had seemed so small in that bucket. But then so had Buddy Sr., when I finally saw his body, and yet it took six men to bear his casket.

"How you reckon she got in that junk yard?" Garth says.

"The usual way," I say. "Except . . . you'd expect her to be *in* one of those cars, like in the trunk. Not in the ground."

"Only a dumbass would leave a body in a trunk," Garth says.

"But why the junk yard? With the Biopark right there?"

He blows a cloud and says, "You're the professor. Maybe the guy figured he'd kill two birds with one stone: get some cash for his junker and get rid a the body. So he puts her in the trunk, hey? Gets the yard to come tow his junker, then walks in there later, finds the car, hauls her out and buries her. Only he don't figure on the Biopark. He don't figure a junk yard is ever gonna go nowhere."

The splotched skin of his brow bunches up, and he appears to snarl. "What?" he says.

"Nothing," I say, going for my beer.

"Nothing my ass."

"I ain't saying how that gal got there," Jimmy says. "But they gone rest her husband, dollars and donuts."

Slowly, with effort, Garth shifts his eyes from mine to Jimmy's. "Dollars *to* donuts, Jimmy. How many times I gotta say it?"

"They gone rest him, Garth. You watch."

"You psychic now, too?"

"Naw," says Jimmy. "That's what happened to my dad. Only he wasn't my real dad. He killed my mom and then they rested him and put him in the prison."

I stare at Jimmy. We both do. I can hear the ceiling fan, the slow, chopperlike *whup whup* of the blades. Garth lights a fresh Camel.

"We known each other about a hundred years, Jimmy, and you never said nothin' like this. You said you was a orphan."

"I was a orphan, Garth. That's how come."

"So how old was you when—you became a orphan."

"Six years eggzact."

"On your birthday, Jimmy?" I say.

"Yes sir. She made me angelfood cake, then he conked her on her head with his Stilson wrench. He wanted a conk me too but I run. I run better'n I walk, sometimes. Plus he was pissed and he fell over my bike. He said he's tire a living with retards. Lady next door called the police, and after that I gone to the orphnage."

"Jesus, Jimmy," says Garth. "Seems like you'da mentioned this before."

"I did. I tole Buddy when he give me my job. I figgerd he tole you."

"No, he never did."

"Huh," says Jimmy.

"Maybe he told Buddy Junior, though," Garth says.

"No," I say. There's a long silence. The *whup whup whup* of the blades. The eyes of the soldiers. "We didn't talk too much."

———

In the end, we are the last to leave. The other dirt men have places to go. Doublewides and girlfriends. Rugrats and Hungry Man dinners. (Do such lives make it easier to forget about a dead girl, or harder? Do any of them know more about her than they're saying? If I stand up, will I fall on my ass?)

"If Buddy could see you now, boy," Garth says, half-grinning.

"Your point?" I say.

"No point, Junior. I was just observing the whattayacallit. Irony."

My head bobs on my neck. "How the mighty have fallen?"

"Naw, son. I never said you was mighty."

"HA!" I say, and a true grin cracks his old face, and he laughs, but then the laugh becomes a series of ripping coughs he tries to catch in his fist. Jimmy waits for the fit to pass, then asks, "OK, Garth?" and Garth nods, red-faced, and tips back his bottle, and something in the folds of his eye catches the light, a speck of water. He wipes his lips with the back of his hand, and as the hand comes down his eyes seem to stumble onto me. Like he wasn't expecting to see me sitting there. "Boy," he says. "What the hell are you doin' here?"

"Here—?" I say, indicating the table, and the old man grunts, and grabs his Camels, and turns away, all his focus on the cigarette, the flame. When he exhales he watches the smoke, nothing else.

After a moment I say, enunciating carefully: "I ran afoul of policy."

Jimmy turns to Garth. "What'd he say?"

"Says he got shit-canned."

"How come you got shit-canned, Junior Buddy?"

"Scomplicated," I say.

"He don't wanna talk about it, Jimmy. He's embarrassed."

"Nothing to be embarrassed about," I say. "Simple misunderstanding." And then, somehow, my mouth keeps going—someone else's tongue in there, bumping against my teeth, making sounds . . . going on about this girl in Colorado, this student, this cowboy boot-wearing, brilliant little thing. A writer of such skill I could never show her essays to the rest of the class, it would have devastated them. It devastated *me*, her talent. And thrilled me. I wanted to teach her, to hone her, but in the end my job was only to guide her toward editors who scooped her up, who were amazed to learn she was just nineteen. The girl, in her youth, went about her days as before, checking her text messages, going to classes, twisting her hair around her finger while my heart beat, while it galloped, for the both of us.

Her final essay began as handsomely as the others, a prose song about helping her father breed horses in the Wind River Mountains. It forayed a while, just a tad sentimentally, through days of home-schooling (when she thought of school playgrounds she felt, she wrote, *far off as a star and just as small*), before bursting out at a dead sprint on the subject of God, and Faith, and the college's determination, by sheer curricular force, to ram the *hypothesis of evolution* down her throat.

The *hypothesis*, she wrote, several times, with the italics, until at last I scrawled in the margin, "Celeste! Why don't you explore this word instead of all this *italicizing*?"

Then, later: "Are you serious, Celeste?"

Understand—prior to this she'd written gorgeously against oil rigs in Alaska. She'd called the V.P. a "grim little Bonaparte." It seemed some trick, a hoax, that this latest could have sprung from the breast of such a girl. I wanted to call up those editors and say *Wait! Do no not publish those essays!*

At the end of that final paper, in disbelief, in heartbreak, I wrote: "Let's meet and talk about this, OK?" I assigned no grade.

At class the next day when the hour was up Celeste didn't linger. She was first out the door, her boot heels scuffing smartly. She didn't show up for the next class, or the one after that. When I called, her roommate told me she was out. She was out and out and out.

I received an e-mail from the Dean. He closed the door and showed me the paperwork, an official document: . . . *intolerance of religious beliefs to the point of harassment, both in written comments and in inappropriate private meetings with the student.*

But Chuck, this is crazy! I burst out. She misunderstood me. She's confused. I'll talk to her—

In fact, Chuck said with a dark look, that would be the last thing you want to do, Buddy, trust me.

Two days later I rode to the dorm and knocked on her door. All I wanted was an explanation—one last, good sentence from my prodigy, my star!

Her roommate wouldn't open the door all the way. She said Celeste had gone home already, to Wyoming. Her phone number, her address—? The roommate made a face. I was standing there in my bike helmet.

Seriously, buddy, she said (or was it Buddy?): you need to get a grip.

Of course, word got back to the Dean, and that was that: my contract was not renewed. My college days were over.

With his free, non-smoking hand, Garth rubs his face. He looks too old for work, all at once, too old even to be drinking at the VFW. He should be home, feeding his cats.

"That is a sorry goddam story, Buddy," he says. His whole face moves around like rubber. "That story's sorrier even than Jimmy's—no offense, Jimmy."

Jimmy shrugs.

Garth releases his face and stares fixedly at his cigarette. And suddenly I get it: the weight loss, the splotched skin, the coughing. It's the cancer. Lungs, maybe throat. Down in him good like oil in dirt, and spreading.

"On the other hand," he says, "maybe they done you a favor. Maybe that wasn't the right line a work for you."

I don't reply, and his face changes, firms up subtly, refreshing my memory on the smug, larky grin I so despised as a kid. "I'm just saying," he says. "If a man can get in that much trouble over a piece a—"

I strike the table with my fist. Eddie the bartender looks over with his eye.

"Steady, Buddy," says Jimmy.

I open my fist and lay it flat on the table to stop the ringing.

"Though I can't say I ever pegged you for a stud horse, Junior," Garth goes on. "But damn, son, you a chip off the old block, ain't you."

I look into his eyes and feel myself spasm, like Jimmy.

"What?" I say.

"What, what? Don't give me that." He stares at me, taking the full tour. "All them girls Buddy hired for the office? You don't remember the girls, Junior? Hell, I do. Jimmy does."

Jimmy does not confirm.

"But, damn it," Garth says in a lower, blacker tone. "He crossed a line with Dolores."

"Dolores . . ." I say.

"Dolores Schotz, Junior. Mrs. Dolores Schotz? The other side of Schotz and Knudson Excavat—"

"Shut up, old man. Shut your trap."

"Don't you talk to me that way, boy. Don't you dare."

Even as we are speaking these words I'm seeing her: Mrs. Schotz. *Dolly*, my parents called her. She was old but her smile burned me up. From my bedroom window I could see them on the back porch, drinking. Sometimes I'd get her profile, her throat when she laughed. Sometimes a bare calf thrown over a knee. *Mrs. Schotz, Dolly Schotz, Dolly*, I'd say, standing at my window . . .

Garth's jowls tremble, and for a moment I think he's going to strike me. For a moment I hope he does.

"Didn't you ever wonder why your momma took off?" he says. "Didn't you ever in all your college days wonder why your old man suddenly up and sold a business he created from nothin' with his bare hands, hey? Did you think it was so you could go off and *hone* your little cowgirls? Is that what you thought?"

By the pounding in my skull, the spin of the room, by how very much I hate him, I know I'm hearing something accurate. The office girls, Dolly Schotz—I'd known but I'd put them away, as Buddy Sr. and I put away whatever might force us to look each other in the eye, to see each other. It was our pact, and it survived the years—was still in effect when he got sick, and didn't say how bad, and I didn't come home to see but stayed at school, chasing down disgrace to its very end while he withered and suffered and died in a hospital bed.

"Where you going?" Garth says. Alerting me to the fact that I've stood up.

"Out," I say.

"Sit down," he says. "You dumb little jerk-off," he says when I'm back in my chair. "You oughta be thanking me."

"Thanking you," I say.

"That's right. You went to college because a me."

Almost nothing from his mouth would shock me, but this is so unexpected, so bizarre that I don't, in fact, believe my ears. I turn to Jimmy, fully expecting to find some confirming expression under that cap. But he won't look up. His big concern is peeling the label from his bottle.

Garth turns his Camel into a pointer. "You think I could just stand by and watch Bill Schotz get done like that, behind his back like that? I knew him way before I knew Buddy, and that is a good man, Bill Schotz. He didn't deserve it, and I told Buddy so—exactly so. Said if he didn't fess up, by God somebody would. And that was the end of Schotz and Knudson. Till you come back."

I glance away—up, at the TV behind the bar. The Biopark is on the screen again, a re-run of earlier footage, the six men carrying that white bag.

"But Bill Schotz was there," I hear myself say. "He carried the casket."

"I know he did, boy. I was next to him."

Also true. Garth was there. Garth, and Bill, and four other men I'd known by name my whole life, including Jimmy Day. Jimmy with his haywire legs and jerking head—a mistake, I remember thinking, a disaster. Yet the casket stayed aloft, and I saw that the other men were bearing Jimmy as much as my father. It had all been understood, and agreed upon, and carried out, without me.

"God damn it, Buddy," Garth says with a new weariness, a jolting quietude in his voice. "Ain't nobody gets off scot-free. Your dad knew it, Jimmy's step-dad knew it, and whoever buried that gal out there is gonna know it before too long. And you know it too, don't you."

I hold his gaze, and I nod, but to what, I'm not sure. He nods back and takes a breath and squares himself, and even Jimmy looks at me with something like approval. Stunning me, in fact, with the disclosure of his eyes, which are as clear and blue as any boy's. I've made some kind of agreement, they are telling me, some kind of promise, the details of which need not be discussed, not tonight, maybe not ever.

Very well. I go for my wallet, but they stop me. They won't hear of it. They are working men, these men, and their pockets are full of cash.

Water

She was a good sleeper, a dependable sleeper, but that night Charlotte woke up with her heart whumping, like a young mother. There had been something.

She lay in the dark, not breathing. At one window the drapes were shaped by faint light from the street, but at the other there was nothing, no light from the neighbors, no moonlight, and the effect was briefly frightening, as if the wall had fallen away into space, or a black sea.

She drew the alarm clock into focus: 1:36. She had a son who would stay out late, but when he came home he was like a cat, and if she heard him at all it was because she had gotten up to use the washroom, pausing by his door just long enough to hear him clicking at the computer in there, or humming to the iPod, or shhshing Ginny Simms, his girl.

She heard none of this now, nothing at all but the heat pumping invisibly, bloodlike, in the walls of the house. This was late October, two nights before Halloween, the first truly cold night of the season.

She closed her eyes and the dream she'd been having eddied back to center—a dream of hands, the feel of them, the smell of them; muscle and tendon, palm and finger. Her body, under the bedding, still hummed. She breathed, she slowed, she drifted down.

And heard it: *Water*.

Water was running in the pipes somewhere. Not the shower, or the toilet, or the kitchen sink: this was the distinctive 1-inch-pipe gush you heard when the boys were washing the truck, or the dog, or filling the plastic pool for the neighbor kids. She had been married to a plumber and she knew about pipes.

She got into her robe and went down the hall, past the boys' rooms—John's door open, no John; Dukie's door shut but him in there, a mound of sleep she could feel like a pulse—and down the stairs to the kitchen, where the noise was loudest.

John's truck was in the window over the sink, lit up by the worklight he used at night, a light usually manned by Dukie but now positioned somewhere out of view, like John. Two yellow smiley faces stared in at her, plastic hoods for the foglights, or whatever they were, he'd mounted on the cab. Her comment on the hoods—*A bit cheesy, John*—was still amusing him, apparently, when he and Dukie carved the identical inane faces into their pumpkins. She'd rolled her eyes but was secretly moved: they'd never done twins before.

Charlotte held her robe to her throat and leaned over the sink. She saw the truck's fender, the tire, a thin disk of water leaching into the gravel, and just then the spigot gave a squeal and the water stopped running and a face popped up before her so suddenly her hands flew up. John saw the movement, then saw her, and Charlotte's heart surged, as if he were hurt, as if he were washing out some great wound she couldn't see. In the next moment she heard the dog, Wyatt, shaking his hide, rattling his tags, and she understood: John would let the dog out in the park, and it would find some other animal's filth, or carcass, to roll in, and later it would stand there grinning under the hose.

The worklight snapped off and in they came, Wyatt shoving past to dive face-first into her carpet, driving his upper body along with his hind legs, first one side, then the other, grunting in ecstasy.

"Wonderful," Charlotte said, and John said, "I'll get a towel," but then just stood there.

"Did you get it all off?" she asked, and he flinched, as if she'd shouted.

"—What?" he said.

Charlotte gestured at the dog. "Did you get it all off?"

John looked at the dog but he wasn't really looking, she could tell; he was thinking of something else altogether. A year out of high school and there were bars he could get into, him and Mike Simms, and some mornings she'd smell the smoke on him like he'd slept in an ashtray. Other mornings she'd smell strawberries and know that Ginny Simms, Mike's younger sister, had been in the house. Charlotte did not approve of such things, of course—but the next thing you knew John was under the sink with his tools, or throwing the football to his brother, or fixing some neighbor kid's bike. A good boy, at the end of the day. A good son.

"I got it all," John said at last, and he turned for the stairs.

Charlotte switched off the lamp and followed.

"Now what are you doing?" she asked, at his door.

He went on shoving clothes into his duffle.

"Gonna go see Cousin Jer for the weekend," he said. "Shoot some birds."

"John," she said. "It's almost two in the morning."

He didn't reply.

"Does he even know you're coming?"

Of course he did, he told her—it was all set up: he'd be at Jer's in an hour, they'd sleep late and then head up to Uncle Martin's cabin. Back Sunday night.

Charlotte was confused and strangely heated, as if she'd done something humiliating.

"And all this is fine with—your boss?" she said, and John paused, they both did, as the idea of Bud Steadman came into the room: his smell of earth and copper, a certain kind of deodorant. His big good face. His hands.

Charlotte saw something on the switch plate, a dark fingerprint, and began to rub it. There'd been a few men over the years but there had been none for several years, and at forty-three, with two grown sons, she'd been ready to believe that all of that was over for her. But it wasn't, not quite. Bud had a nineteen-year-old daughter at home, Caroline, who didn't get along with her mother—or any older woman, so far as Charlotte could see—and the going was slow. But it was going. When the phone rang these days Charlotte's heart jumped. New bras and panties bloomed in her bureau. She'd lost weight.

The only reason John was out late tonight, with work in the morning, was because she and Bud had made plans for tomorrow night—Friday night, a date—and John had agreed to stay home with his brother.

"I'll call Bud in the morning," he now said. "Mike will cover for me."

"And me?" Charlotte all but yelped, swatting him lightly. "We had a deal!"

He shrank from her.

"You can still go out, Ma. I'll take Big Man with me."

"Oh, you will, will you? Hunting?" She stared at him, waiting for one of the Duke's howls to fill his head; most recently, it had been the torn heap of rabbit at Wyatt's feet. A smashed jack-o'-lantern could do the job.

"You got a point," John said.

A moment passed. The dog was on the bed, on its back, twisting and snorting as if in agony.

Charlotte shook her head. *Uff da!* her grandmother would say, venting the woe from her old Norwegian heart. The same pressure would build in Charlotte but she resisted, remembering the farm in Minnesota: Granddad pulling her off some piece of machinery with a swat; Grammy Moore whacking the neck of a chicken—the jetting blood, the headless, frantic life that didn't want to end. *Nothing in this life comes easy,* Charlotte had been told, and though it turned out to be true, she'd never said the same to her own children, in case it was the saying so that made it so.

She shook her head, she sighed. She would see Bud Steadman in the morning, at the Plumbing & Supply. A change of plans, she'd say. Home-cooked dinner instead. She'd get Dukie to turn in early. Like her, that boy was a sleeper.

But Bud Steadman wasn't at the Plumbing & Supply in the morning, his van wasn't there, and Charlotte followed the sullen Dukie into the store with something childish, something ridiculous and acute jabbing at her heart.

"Big Man!" Mike Simms called as they came in, and the Duke raised his hand for a gustoless high-five, then disappeared into the back, stranding Charlotte with no good-bye. It was her fault John had gone off to the cabin without him, was the message.

She stood there a moment amongst the pipes and fittings. The smell of the place was a smell she loved: pipe dope and PVC glue and sweated copper and men. She remembered the summer when Bud and Raymond had bought the building and began fixing it up. Sawdust in the nostrils, freckles of paint on all their faces. Charlotte and Meredith had fallen for each other like schoolgirls, the kind of gushy, overnight friendship men don't even try to understand. They both got pregnant the same month, and then, five months later, when Charlotte and Raymond learned there was trouble with the twins—one healthy, one not; they could terminate one to save one, or risk losing both—it was Meredith and Bud who loaned them money for more tests, a second opinion, the monitoring that saved John's life. He had his heart murmur, but he'd grown strong as a lion. And the Duke, well, the Duke was the Duke . . . No one had seen that coming.

Six years later, Raymond was dead. The cancer they'd been fighting in one lung had jumped to the other like a clever rat. Charlotte had to give up the business to keep the house. She and Meredith's friendship began to falter, and she realized that after all it was the men, not the women, who kept the two families close. She heard through other friends about Meredith's miscarries, but only called after the first. Both had been boys, she heard.

Then, when her own sons were sixteen, here came Bud again, with jobs: custodial duties for Dukie and the secrets of the trade for John. Bud had never gotten around to changing the Steadman-Moore sign on the side of the building, and a hyphen that had once said *family* to Charlotte, then *loss* (a minus sign), then *another lifetime*, suddenly said *family* again.

Now Charlotte asked Mike Simms if he knew when Bud would be back, and the boy replied cheerfully, "Can't say, Mizz Moore. He ain't been in yet."

"Oh," she said, puzzled—actually bothered by this answer.

"Anything I can help you with, Mizz Moore?"

And there it was: Mike Simms had opened up the store. Bud had given him keys.

She'd thought John was the only one.

———

In her car again, driving across town to the mall where she works. A brilliant, stunning blue day in October. Cars moving along in their lanes, catching the light. On the radio two women are talking in quiet tones: one has written a book about her childhood, her abusive drunken father, but it's the women's voices, more than the subject, that takes Charlotte back in time, to a night when she felt friendship land on her like a blow. They had all been working on the store and now she and Meredith sat alone on the deck with the wine. If they were pregnant, they didn't yet know it. The bellies of insects pulsed green in the dusk. Bud had taken Raymond to the basement to talk about turning it into something called a game room. The women could hear the low, manly voices down there.

When she was sixteen, Meredith said, refilling Charlotte's glass, then her own, she had slept with a teacher at her high school.

Charlotte picked up her glass. Took a sip. In her stomach she felt as if a notorious man had just grinned at her.

What kind? she asked. Of teacher.

Art. Mr. Beckman. Mr. B. He thought Meredith had talent. She thought he was a fairy. Everyone did. He passed her one day in his car, an Oldsmobile. She was wearing her best skirt.

Meredith was quite a bit smaller than Charlotte, tiny in fact, with the most extraordinary skin. At sixteen, Charlotte could not even imagine.

They talked about Dali, Meredith said. They parked. He had a mustache that tickled. He wanted to see her again. He stood behind her in class, as she drew. He began slipping her these little drawings—very good, very dirty. An artistic fever, he said into her ear. She showed the drawings to just one person, her best friend, but that was enough. A substitute teacher came to Mr. B.'s art room one day, and stayed. The school was talking. Meredith's father heard it at the plant from some other kid's father, came home and slapped the living crap out of her.

My God, Meredith. Charlotte put her fingers on her friend's cool forearm.

Her dad had these brothers, Meredith continued after a moment in the same quiet, factual tone. Five of them. One, Uncle Donny, was a piece of work. In and out of jail, drunk at Christmas, fuck this and fuck that. About a month after the Mr. B. scandal, Uncle Donny came by the house. He was there just a minute, barely said hello, and two days later they found Mr. B. walking along the interstate. His head was cracked. His teeth were gone. All his fingers were broken.

Laughter came to them from the house, from the basement, making them both turn to stare. Meredith raised her glass again and Charlotte heard it clink lightly against her teeth.

She waited for the cops to come, Meredith said. She stopped eating. She typed a letter at school and sent it anonymously. No one ever came. No one ever did. Mr. B. was in the hospital a long time but he couldn't recognize you, they said, so what was the point of going up there? His parents came and took him away, finally, like a child.

My God, Meredith, Charlotte said again. She could barely see her friend in the dark. Her heart was beating with pity and love. After a while she said, What do you *do* with that?

There was no reply. A long, unnatural soundlessness, a black well of listening. Fireflies like little bombs going off at a great distance. Men coming up the stairs, loud and huge. Meredith's eyes flashed and she said: You bury it, Charlotte.

⁂

The morning passed. Charlotte in the back room tagging sweaters amidst tinny bursts of ring tone from the jackets and purses of the salesgirls. At ten o'clock she walked to the far end of the mall, all the way to the restrooms and the building's—maybe the world's—last payphone. (The little cellphone John and Dukie had given her for her birthday—"Look, it takes pictures!"—sat dead in a kitchen drawer, next to the dead camera.) She intended to call Bud, tell him the new plan, but at the last moment she dialed John's cellphone instead, got his voicemail.

"John, here. You know what to do."

She asked him to leave her a message at home, just to say he arrived at Cousin Jer's OK, then she hung up and began the long walk back to work. She would call Bud later, at her lunch break. It was Friday, and they had a date.

Back at the store, something had happened. Alicia stood alone on the sales floor, thin arms folded over her thin stomach. Ten years younger than Charlotte, she would talk about things like chakras and third eyes and orgasms.

Now she came from behind the register as if Charlotte were some girl with an Anne Klein blouse stuffed up her shirt. In the door of the back room Charlotte saw two salesgirls, head-down and furiously texting. *OMG*, said their shoulders, their thumbs.

"There's been an accident," said her boss, and the store rolled and Charlotte pitched backwards, sickly, into a scene on the highway, John's truck inverted on the shoulder, wheels to the sky, black smoke spiraling—

"No, no," Alicia said quickly, "not that, not one of yours. It's Caroline," she said. "Bud Steadman's girl," she said. "They found her this morning in the river."

⚬⚬⚬

The story was going around, cellphone to cellphone: Caroline had been walking home from her boyfriend's. No, she was walking home from the bars. She was alone; she was not alone. She'd been drinking. She was high. The girl had problems—she'd lost her license to a DUI the year before, that much was a fact. She was cutting through the park, along the river, and had fallen in. Jumped in. Been pushed in. She'd been there all night. Someone crossing the bridge had seen her, wallowing against the concrete piling below like driftwood.

Charlotte was in her car again, driving across town. A brilliant, cold blue day. On the sidewalk a young woman with long black hair drew a kite-tail of small children behind her. A man in tights ran by them, smiling. The sun, the blazing trees, the silvered bend of river, all exactly as it should be on a day in October, a pristine day. She tried to picture it: Caroline Steadman, this girl she'd known since birth, floating in the water with the branches. But all Charlotte saw clearly was the blouse, the one she'd given the girl on her nineteenth birthday, Bud looking on uneasily: a smart, semi-sheer blouse she'd spent too much on, even with her discount, all night in the river under the black sky, the fabric wetted to skin except where air slipped in, raising white, tremulous welts on the water.

"Charlotte—"

He was startled, confused to see her. His pale face, the bruised unfocussing eyes, swept away anything she might've been ready to say.

"I'm sorry," she said, "I tried to call first . . ." Three times, from the store—three times got his voicemail, three times hung up. What was the message you left for this? *Go*, Alicia said finally. *He's going to need you.*

But he was not asking her in, or even letting go of the storm door so she could put her arms around him. She wasn't surprised, she told herself, certainly not hurt—it had nothing to do with her. He had to handle things his own way, in his own time.

"I'm so sorry, Bud," she said into those eyes.

"They took me to her," he said. "The police. To make sure."

"Oh, Bud. By yourself?"

He didn't answer, he seemed to be listening, and she listened too: someone else in the house, on the phone. A voice of calm male authority. She glanced at the extra car in the drive, a black spotless Lexus.

"Someone's with you?"

"Duncan."

"That's good. That's good, Bud." His brother Duncan, she remembered, was some kind of lawyer for the state. She'd met him once and had been struck by the cleanliness of his fingernails, a thing she was not used to in men.

"Can I do anything, Bud, is there anything I can do?"

He caught her eyes, fleetingly, possibly by accident. He said, "Meredith's on her way. Her sister's driving her down. I thought it was them when you knocked."

Charlotte nodded, but couldn't speak. She hadn't seen Meredith in years, not since before the divorce. She remembered that night on the deck, with the wine, when her heart had filled with pity and love. They were going to be friends forever, old ladies, arm in arm in Mexico, Europe, after the husbands were gone. When the first crack in their friendship appeared, not long after Raymond's death, it was that story again, that secret—Mr. B.—that somehow widened the crack and made it permanent.

"They think now maybe she didn't just drown," Bud said abruptly.

"They—?" said Charlotte.

"The police." He dug at the black and gray whiskers on his face. "They think someone hit her with a car."

"My God." Charlotte had the sensation of dropping through space, her stomach rising.

"They think this person didn't see her maybe," Bud said. "Then tried to cover it up by pushing her in the river. Can't be sure," Bud said, "but it looks like she was still alive, then. When they pushed her in. Looks like she was still breathing."

<hr />

"Mama," Dukie said when she came in, "the police men was here. One man and one girl police man." He was at the plate glass window, spritzing away smears and fingerprints. Mike Simms sat behind the counter, unsmiling. Charlotte looked at him and he nodded.

"They're going around talking to people," he said. "Anyone who mighta seen her last night."

Charlotte nodded, too. She thought a moment. She tried to think. She had meant to ask Mike about John, if they'd been together last night, but now she didn't want to look at him again. She couldn't seem to breathe.

"Dukie, get your jacket," she said, lifting her purse to dig in it, though her keys were already in her hand.

"Gotta do windows, Mama."

"Tomorrow, Dukie. Today's a short day."

At home she was barely in the door, had barely glanced at the answering machine—no blinking red light, nothing—before she saw the car outside, in the street. A plain blue sedan parked as if it had been there all day, when she knew it hadn't been there just seconds ago. Two men in ties and jackets were coming toward the house. She met them at the door, and the taller of the two, calling himself Detective Carson, watched her face as he made sure Charlotte was aware of the unfortunate news regarding . . . while the other man, Detective Something, brushed past her with his eyes and began tearing the house apart.

They were trying to learn as much as they could about the night before, this Carson was explaining. They understood that her son John had been at the bar where Caroline was last seen alive.

Charlotte wasn't sure if this was a question, but she said she couldn't say about that, she didn't know where he'd been.

The other man, chewing gum, stopped, and resumed chewing. He looked and sounded as if his mouth had been invaded by some small creature.

After a moment—after Carson asked—she let them in.

There wasn't much she could tell them, as there wasn't much she knew, and just a few minutes after they left she had trouble remembering their names, their faces, trouble believing they were ever there at all. She tried to call John again. Kept trying until she heard, from her brother Martin, calling her, that he was in custody. They'd found him up at the cabin, and there was no trouble.

"In custody—?" Charlotte heard herself say.

"Not arrested," her brother said quickly. "Not charged."

"But in custody," Charlotte said.

There's a gray area, he told her—and he went on reassuring her, but Charlotte's mind was tumbling. She was at the kitchen window, as she had been the night before. Two yellow eyes looking in the window, the twin smiley-faces. Water, she remembered. The dog had rolled in something. She saw her son's face, the gust of white breath when he saw her in the window.

There was nothing out there now. No truck. No son.

In custody.

———

It's dark when tires crunch in the drive, and she quickly turns off the TV. A car door slams, the tires crunch the gravel again, and in walks John. Charlotte is up from the sofa but everything about him says *Stop, don't touch me.* Dukie comes in and lifts him in a bear hug until John says "Put me down, idiot."

"John," Charlotte says.

He ignores her, going for the stairs.

"Hey, where's Wyatt?" Dukie bellows.

"I had to leave him up there, with Jer."

"Oh, no!" cries Dukie.

"Who brought you home?" Charlotte asks, afraid to hear the answer—that it was those men, the detectives—and John stops on the stairs.

"Why are you even here, Ma?"

Charlotte stares at him.

"Why aren't you on your *date?*"

"John—" she says again, with purpose, but then falters. She has a feeling of choking, of drowning. His eyes burn into her a moment, then he turns again, and the two of them, her boys, disappear over the rise of the stairs.

She locks the doors and closes drapes. It crosses her mind to pull the phone line from the wall, and in that instant the phone rings.

It's Martin again, her brother. There's nothing for her to worry about, he says, he's been talking to the lawyer. He spends some time telling her things she hardly hears, something about physical evidence, the phrase "erratic, troubled girl," and Charlotte mechanically takes down the number of the lawyer.

There's a silence, and she asks, "Do you think he knows?"

"Who?" Martin says.

"Bud Steadman. Do you think he knows . . . about John?"

"You haven't talked to him?"

"Yes, earlier. Briefly. He wasn't—he . . ." She doesn't finish.

"He's a good man, Char," Martin says. "And he's been good to those boys. But what he's going through right now . . . Hell, I don't even want to imagine."

She waits for the detectives to return, but they don't—not that night, not all day Saturday.

She waits for Bud to call, although she knows that won't happen either, not as long as those cars are parked in his drive— the black Lexus, and now a white Volvo she knows is the car Meredith came down in.

And then it's Sunday night, Halloween. John emerges from his room at last, on his way to Mike Simms' waiting truck, and off they go. Charlotte sits home with the Duke, who sits in his

Packers helmet and jersey, ready to dish out candy for kids if any come. None do; not one. It's a bad night for it, a bitter wind blowing, so no wonder.

Later, after Dukie's gone to bed, something sails through the living room window and lands on the carpet. A small stone out of the sky. It's surprising what a clean, small hole it makes, with only a few slender shards to pick up. The pieces are still in her hand when the phone rings.

"Hello?" she says. *"Hello—?"*

"Hello? Mrs. Moore?"

Mrs. Moore! The blood goes out of her, she steadies herself on the counter.

But it isn't him, it isn't Bud. It's his brother, Duncan.

Charlotte manages to give her sympathies, then listens while Duncan explains that Bud isn't going to open the store tomorrow, so the boys should plan on staying home.

"Of course," Charlotte says. She sees the scene over there, at Bud's house: Duncan at the phone and Bud beyond him, heaped in a chair, staring into coffee, Meredith on the sofa, their daughter, their only child, dead.

"But I wonder," she says, "is there any chance—"

"In fact," says the brother, "they should probably plan on staying home until further notice, Mrs. Moore."

After he hangs up, Charlotte keeps the phone to her ear, listening to the strange, enormous silence there, a sound from the windy blacks of space. She stands frozen in it, her chest emptied. There was a day, years ago, when something happened, or nearly happened, between her and Bud Steadman. A gray afternoon, the window panes ticking with bits of ice. She had come out of a bath and felt weak and had sat down on the bed. Before her was the cheval glass that had belonged to her grandmother, her mother, now her. Who would she give the mirror to, this girly keepsake?

Charlotte—?

A man in the house, downstairs. Her heart gave a kick.

His footfall across the living room, and then her name again, lobbed up the stairs. A stair tread creaked and she reached for her robe, but stopped.

Two days ago they had buried Raymond. This afternoon, Bud had picked up the boys and taken them to a movie so Charlotte could sleep. Now they were back.

Charlotte—? he said from around the corner.

Yes, she answered. That was all. He came anyway, into the frame of the door.

Oh—His big face filled with the shock of her there, on the bed. I'm sorry, he said.

She heard kids in the yard, boys and girls, already into some kind of contest. Caroline could be mean but John would keep things fair and good for the Duke.

Brought the boys back, Bud said, not looking away, looking her in the eye. He reached up and worked the flesh under his jaw with a coarse, sandpaper sound. He was a man who was sure before he acted, who didn't operate by guesswork or even intuition, but who held in his head all the hard facts of mechanical things. Over the years there had been moments, yes, when she'd wondered what it would be like to be with him instead of Raymond, to simply switch. Innocent, helpless thoughts such as every woman must have . . .

He took a step, then came certainly toward her. In the wash of movement she smelled the outdoors, the steely clouds and the wet, moldering leaves. Green buttons rode the flannel wave of his stomach down to his belt. The buckle was a little brass mouth with a little brass tongue. Her heart beat in her breast. She turned to the mirror and the picture there was incredible: this naked, wet-haired woman, this man beside her dressed for cold—the forward cant of his body, the emptiness of his hands.

Charlotte—he said, and in the next instant Caroline's voice, shrill and imperious, penetrated the room like a wind.

Hands off, retard!

Out there, in the cold, John said something low, and silence followed. Bud's face was crimson. His jaw muscle jumped.

She knows better, by God.

It's all right, Charlotte said.

The day was going dark. In the mirror she saw Bud's arm drift toward her shoulder, then beyond it. She saw her robe rise up like a spirit, felt it brush her shuddering skin. In the mirror, as in the flesh, he got the robe over her shoulders and over her breasts without quite touching her.

There is glass in her hand, Charlotte notices, standing at the sink. Slender fragments pressed into her palm, and after a moment she remembers the broken window, the strange little stone. She dumps the glass in the trash and rinses her hand under the faucet. She had wanted to tell him something, that day—something true and unafraid, such as how she'd often felt, her secret thoughts. Caroline's voice had stopped her.

And if it hadn't? If everything had gone just a little bit differently? Meteors, they said, were on their way, right now, crossing billions of years of chance. If Caroline had not spoken and Charlotte had—would things be different? Would Caroline be alive?

It's late, almost midnight. Wind is moaning in a gap some-where. She begins going around the rooms locking doors, switching off lights. She's halfway up the stairs before she remembers John is still out, but she doesn't go back down to turn on the lamp. In a few weeks, he'll be gone. He'll take off one day while she's at work, leaving just a note saying he's gone down to St. Louis, to work construction with a friend of his. The lawyer will call a few days later looking for him—John's cellphone number no longer works—but it's a social call, mainly, just checking in. John's a good kid, the lawyer will say before hanging up. Charlotte raised a good boy.

Not long after that she will see that Bud Steadman has finally changed the sign on the side of the building—white-washing out the hyphen and everything after—and that's when she'll decide to go, too. Her father still has the farm in Minnesota, where as a girl she learned nothing comes easy. It's a place, a life, she had left behind. But you never do. There's room for her and Dukie and the dog, Wyatt, which John has left behind. The first time she cooks for him, at the old stove, her father weeps.

John will come up for Thanksgiving and Christmas that first year, then just Christmas, then not even that. One day Charlotte will get a card in the mail, two photos inside. Here is her new daughter-in-law, Cheryl; here is her grandson, Grant—the very image of John and Dukie when they were born. But "healthy," John writes, "and normal."

When the dog finally dies—of cancer, like Raymond— Charlotte decides to call her son. She's remembering the day he found the dog, just this bag of bones down by the tracks. He'd fed it some licorice and when he turned to go it latched its jaw onto his calf muscle. Seeing the teeth marks in his skin—the skin unbroken, thank God—Charlotte got up to call the pound, the Board of Health, the police. But John had looked at her, and then at Dukie, who was studiously petting the animal's skull.

This was late November, maybe December. Raymond had not been dead very long.

John kneeled next to his brother and began stroking the dog's ragged spine. You know what they'll do to him, he said quietly, as if to himself.

What? said the Duke. What will they do to him?

Don't, Charlotte said. John, don't . . .

Well. He had been a good dog, after all. Smart, happy, devoted to John as if he'd never forgotten that piece of licorice, that sudden change of fortune. After John left, leaving him behind with Charlotte and Dukie, he was not the same animal. His heart was broken. Sickness saw an opening.

"What do you want me to do with him, John?" she now asks on the phone, her voice under control. It was the water, she remembers—the sound of water in the pipes. If he had never turned it on she would never have come downstairs. She would never have seen him out there with the hose in his hand, would never have seen the look on his face the moment he knew she was there, the moment he knew he'd been seen.

Of course, if she had not had a date with Bud Steadman—if she had never had feelings for Bud Steadman—John would not have been out at all that night. This is Charlotte's final thought on the matter, again and again, up there in Minnesota.

"What else can you do?" John says at last on the phone, in the voice of an older man, a husband, a father. "You bury him, Ma."

Things Go Missing

Part I: Malfeasance

For a while, there, I was a burglar. I mean I walked uninvited into people's homes and took their things and kept them for myself—though usually not for very long. My locker would fill up and girls would notice, the way girls do, and if they saw something they liked I'd either give it to them or take some cash just for appearances—two bucks for a near-empty bottle of N°5, five for something really desirable like a red alligator clutch. If anybody asked, it was all stuff my mother was getting rid of. When business got too brisk, or I began to recognize too many things in the halls, I'd start ditching my haul before I got back to school, or else I'd take it home and stash it in my mother's boxes in the attic, knowing that Dad, if he ever went up there, would not be able to tell the difference.

Say "burglar" and people think: Male, full-grown, night-time, black clothes, flashlight. They don't think: Girl, ponytail, pancake chest, Gap jeans—ringing the bell in the middle of the day, asking, *Is Betty-Lynn home—?* No kid was *ever* named Betty-Lynn. And no nanny, or full-time mom, or hooky-playing teen, ever remembered the likes of me ten minutes later.

Mostly, though, no one was home. The neighborhoods I could reach by bike during lunch period were a long commute from the city, where almost everybody worked during the days. And maybe it was that commute, all those protective miles between home and city, that made people sloppy when it came to home security. (As for Hide-A-Key rocks: Easter eggs are harder to spot. As for watchdogs: even the meanest go to pieces at the first taste of Oreo.) The moment I was in, my heart would begin to whump and I'd hear a certain high note in my ears, but I was never afraid, and I never rushed. If my shoes were dirty I took them off at the door. Before I helped myself to a Coke from the fridge I made sure it wasn't the last one. If I turned on a light I always turned it off again. And when I got to the master bedrooms, with their densely, privately scented atmospheres, their wide-open closets and still-damp bathrooms, their little cities of lotions and perfumes, I became even more patient, though my heart kicked on my ribs. I had to find just the right kind of thing—nothing so expensive or wonderful that anyone would ever think to call the police or fire the housecleaner. I didn't want to cause the women I stole from anything more than a few minutes of head-scratching: things go missing, that's all, let's move on.

Although, I learned the hard way, women can be touchy about just about anything.

A girl named Reagan Dudziak—not a queen herself, exactly, but never far from that hive—had given me three dollars for a pair of open-toe platform clogs she thought were hilarious. She painted up her toenails and wore the clogs to school the next day and everybody could hear her coming like a Clydesdale. The boys took note and teams of jealous girls tracked her all day, and that night she called me—me, Josephine Kelso!—and talked for almost five minutes before she got another call and had to go. By Friday, Reagan had touched off a craze of clogwear that got so thunderous Principal Fennerman was forced to ban them from the school dress code, and it was this outrageous act, finally, that got the attention of Reagan's mother, the lawyer.

The Monday after the clog ban, Reagan came up to me (stealthily, in hot-pink Sketchers) and demanded to know where I'd gotten those clogs in the first place, since it seems they were identical to a pair her mother had worn in the seventies and which, after an all-out upside-down Saturday-ruining search of the house, were totally missing, and so now her mother thought she was *lying* to her!

I smiled and felt sick as I saw any hope of friendship with Reagan Dudziak snatched away like a note. There was nothing to do but stick to my story about the clogs belonging to my mother—with the impromptu twist that she'd bought them at the Salvation Army the Halloween before as part of her disco costume. Whereupon, wordlessly, Reagan called me a freak and walked away. I knew she wouldn't call again, but for days afterward I kept close to the phone, slick-palmed, in case her mother did, in case I had to pretend to be mine.

The Reagan Dudziak Incident taught me to crosscheck the addresses of my classmates against the addresses of the houses I burgled, and I learned never to boost anything that looked older than I was or might otherwise have some kind of retro-appeal to classmates, since such items tended to have values to older women way beyond the comprehension of anyone who wasn't, herself, an older woman.

———

I'm not proud of the burgling, and I never was. It was never about getting away with something, or doing something bad, or even about possessions. In the beginning, it was about cake. I was ten, and the boy next door had shown me a key he wasn't supposed to, and I wanted a hunk of his leftover birthday cake, and so I watched from our window until the whole family drove off, then I walked over there and got my cake, and after that I went upstairs and jumped on Mrs. Baxter's bed, and I took a pee in her toilet, and I tried on, but did not steal, some of her rings, and nobody ever knew a thing about it, and for some reason this appealed to me. I never expected to make a habit of it. Who would?

But almost anything, in time, can get to seem like nothing. And it didn't amaze me at all when I got busted, finally, not for breaking into people's homes, but for telling lies.

Someone, somehow—perhaps it was Reagan Dudziak and her lawyer mother—figured out I'd been lying nonstop about my mother for the entire time I'd been in middle school (she was a Fed-Ex pilot; she was on a tomb dig in Egypt; she was inoculating babies in the Congo), and I was summoned from math class one day to meet with School Nurse Luske. The year before, it was School Nurse Luske who explained to all us girls, in a special one-hour humor-free assembly, the special arithmetic of boys and bleeding and impregnation. In private, it turned out, Nurse Luske was more gentle and human—she knew all about Mom, and Dad, and even a little about Roxanne, my sister—and I wanted to cooperate. But each time Nurse Luske paused to let me speak, her assembly-voice boomed on in my head:

STIMULATION
OVULATION
EJACULATION
INSEMINATION

and I couldn't hear to think, and so I didn't speak. Which in retrospect was a mistake: now not only was my lying a matter of school record, but so was my attitude. A call was made, and when I got home that afternoon Dad stopped hanging Sheetrock and we had a good father-daughter ten minutes together (me all the while wanting nothing so much as to brush the white dust from his eyebrows), before he went back to the basement and I went up to the attic to dig through boxes until I found Mom's winter jacket, a knee-length white suede overcoat with red satin lining.

I buttoned it up and pressed the collar to my face and smelled it, *smelled it*, until it almost knocked me over. I could feel all the empty space inside the coat, as if Mom had been this Amazon, or else I was just this stick thing, this scarecrow girl—but what I saw in the glass of the window looked so much like her I threw off the coat and went shooting down the stairs, all the way to the basement.

Back at school, after a dispatch went out about my lying, life got harder; it was not so easy to slip away at lunch and burgle houses, nor to unload things on my classmates, including fictions about my mother. Meanwhile, hanging over my head was the three-way pact between Nurse Luske and Principal Fennerman and Dad to send me, in the event of further trouble, to *"see"* a professional. Apparently there was something alarming, even scary, about a girl who liked people to think her mother wasn't dead.

About the only person left in that school who didn't treat me like I was wired for explosives was Jack, the study hall monitor. Not really a full-grown man but not one of these boys, either, Jack was on loan from the community college; he was getting some kind of credit for sitting in the auditorium and reading books while kids took naps and made out and pounded on each other all through his study hall. He had this long, light-catching hair he kept stashed behind his ears, and if you got close enough you could smell it—a scalpy, wooly, gouged-wood smell, as if in his spare time he chopped down trees. *Lumber Jack*, I sometimes said to myself.

One day I came to the auditorium early and found Jack rooting in his pack. He lifted the same big novel three times, patted his shirt pocket, touched his face like a blind man and looked under his chair. He saw me and waved me over.

You see my glasses around here, Jo? I went to the men's room and now I can't find them.

My stomach caved at the thought that, without his glasses, he wouldn't want to talk to me today. Usually I parked myself at his table in front of the stage, and we'd talk about Stephen King and Edgar Allen Poe, and he'd tell me about books I should read, and I'd studiously enter them in my notebook. One time, he handed me a book of stories by John Gardner and told me to read "The King's Indian," a ghost story, and to this day it makes me shiver to remember. The handing of the book, I mean.

I started looking around. Didja leave 'em in the men's room?

I don't take them in there with me. He said Shit and tucked his hair behind his ears. I think somebody stole them.

I couldn't imagine that. What would anybody want with a guy's reading glasses?

Probably just a prank, Jack, I said.

He squinted at me. Think so?

Happens all the time.

He thought a moment. Tell you what, Jo. You turn them up for me, and I will give you that John Gardner book.

(Now, my question to you is this: Did Jack know then about my lying? Was I, after all, just another pitiful kid, desperate for attention?)

Well. I jumped on the task. And it didn't take long—oh man was I brilliant! A brilliant idiot.

Under the stage, I told him.

In the base of the stage was a kind of hatch which was supposed to be locked but which everybody knew would open with a good yank of the knob. The math books of popular girls ended up under there, flung by athletic, red-faced boys.

Probably somebody threw them in there as a joke, I said.

Jack looked at me. Then tried the hatch, then moved aside to let me. The hatch rattled open with a suck of cold air and dust motes, and we stooped to peer down a short length of gritty concrete narrowing fast into darkness. The idea of going in there got my blood pumping, like burgling—but not like that: this had ice in it, and the taste of pennies, and little neck spiders.

Still, if he'd asked . . .

He didn't. He gave me a hall pass to go find the janitor. And sister, I *ran*.

Two round lenses winked back at the janitor's flashlight, and the old guy crab-walked in after them.

Jack held his glasses to the light, then sat down to give them a serious cleaning on his flannel shirt. By now the auditorium was full of kids, but I stayed put, pretending to have a hangnail. Finally Jack looked up. He made a face like, *Oh, right*, and began poking around in his pack. Sorry, he said without looking up again. I don't have that book with me today. I'll try to remember it tomorrow.

I sat down feeling sick but telling myself he was probably too upset, just then, to deal with me. Jack was a sensitive guy.

Next period, as I was putting the finishing stitches into an oven mitt that was supposed to be a fish but looked more like a snake, one of the secretaries handed Mr. Fitzpatrick a note, and I went up to see Principal Fennerman.

I understand you helped Mr. Bibby find his glasses today, he began.

Mr. Bibby—?

Jack Bibby, the study hall monitor, he said.

Outside the window a blackbird sailed over Mr. Fennerman's head like a hand grenade. I thought of Jack and his glasses, and the books he would never hand me, and these tears came bursting out of me—spurting through my fingers, spatting down on my thighs like hot rain. I just couldn't stop them!

Mr. Fennerman observed this for a while, then sent for School Nurse Luske.

And from there, almost directly, to Mary Wintermantle.

∞

PART II: Restoration

"Do you smoke, Josephine?"

These were her first words to me, once we were alone in that little office of hers above the pizza parlor. It was a freakishly cold day for October yet the window next to where she sat in her wing-back chair was wide open—to give the sausage and onion smell a way out, I assumed. The fat cinnamon candle on the desk behind her, caved and dripping like a bloody lip, only made things worse, somehow, like certain so-called "freshening" scents in bathrooms.

I was sunk, sitting, in her plump apricot sofa, an accent pillow clamped to my chest, sucking down a glass of water. Despite the open window I felt waves of oven heat rising up through the floor, drying me out like a plant. So it's come to this, I thought: I am one of *those* kids. The ones they wring their hands over. The ones they hope can be fixed by professionals, by drugs. For some kids it happened overnight: back-talking monsters one day, mute little automatons the next. How happy the teachers were to see the change! How horrified were the rest of us!

I said "No," answering her question, and figured it was a good start, for it was no lie; smoking was a bad habit.

"Bravo for you," said Mary Wintermantle, genuinely. "I started when I was your age and I've been a smokestack ever since. Wouldn't quit even to have kids, so I never had them, which is probably how I ended up counseling them. In any case I hope you won't mind . . ." she placed a skinny brown cigarette in her lips and raised a silver Zippo ". . . I will direct my exhaust to the window as best I can."

Within ten seconds of meeting her I learned that my shrink was a childless tobacco addict who liked to talk about herself, and as she lit up I took further stock: her poufy yellow hair with the black roots; the granny glasses depending from her slightly chubby neck; her silk blouse button-strained by bosoms I had a hard time not staring at. She wore a camel hair blazer over the blouse but from the hips down she was all Levis and Reeboks; she was a professional, boy, but she was down home, too. She had her framed documents clustered together on the wall, but there were also photographs of horses, and on the wall directly behind her, between a pair of bookshelves, was a poster of Michael Jordan in ungodly flying pre-dunk. If I were burgling this office, I mused, I could get away with a horse picture, maybe a diploma—definitely not Mike.

"Do you play basketball?" asked Mary, startling me. Whatever else she was doing, I realized—tamping her cigarette, sipping her coffee, drawing horses on her notepad—she was watching me.

"Me? Ha. Rox did, though. Rox was my sister. Is, I mean."

"Why'd you say was?"

"It just slipped."

"She doesn't play anymore?"

"No." And I told her how Roxanne had been the star point guard at her high school, but then how, after our mother died, she began hanging out with the wrong sorts of kids, Dad said, and started smoking, and not coming home at night. I told her how Dad would sit there at dinner, just the two of us, and just stare at his French toast. Sometimes we'd hear a noise in the house, a creak, and he'd look up, with this look, like he thought—

I stopped, and Mary watched me for a few seconds. Then she got up, took the empty glass from me, refilled it from the pitcher, gave it back, and sat down again. Somehow, it was the nicest thing in the world.

"So then what happened? Josephine?"

"So, then . . . Dad decided we needed to move. If we moved out of that school district, then Rox would stop hanging out with those kids. Went the theory."

"And how did you feel about that?"

I twitched. I did this spazzy thing I sometimes did when a teacher said my name out of the blue, reminding me where I was, who I was.

"Um," I said. "I don't know. I guess I thought he was right, that it was the best way."

"But didn't you have friends too?"

"Sure, you know. But whatever. Roxanne was like, seriously . . ." I trailed off into silence, and Mary let me go. Puffed on her cigarette. I wanted to steal a glance at the little crystal clock behind her on the desk but didn't think I could pull it off.

"So, then what. Rox left home?"

"Is that in my file or something?"

"I don't have a file on you, we just met."

"Yeah, she left. She's somewhere in the city, we think."

"I'm sorry, Josephine."

I shrugged. "Stuff happens."

"It surely does. My Dad kicked me out of the house when I was seventeen for dating a basketball player. Guess who."

I looked at the poster.

"No way."

"Way, sister. He dumped me when he went to N.C., but he still wrote me letters, time to time."

"Are you still, like—" (Is that why she'd come to Chicago?)

"In love with the guy? Naw. It fades. Now I just love to watch him play. Or did, anyway. What a creature!" She shook her poufy hair. "But you shoulda seen my dad's face, watching Mike on TV—the conflict, the anguish!"

And so passed my first hour with Mary Wintermantle, a funny blend of my sob stories cake-layered with hers, until we were interrupted by a timid rap on the door.

"What the hell?" she said, rising. It was Dad.

"Sorry," he began, "I've been out here a while, I didn't know if I was supposed to just wait or what." There were these little nodes of what looked like oatmeal on the lenses of his glasses. He'd begun spraying the basement ceiling at home.

"Hello, Mr. Kelso. We were just wrapping up. But next time do please wait for us to come out, all right?"

"Oh. All right. I'm very sorry."

"Hush. Now—may I see your glasses a second?"

Dad looked confused but didn't really hesitate. He handed them over and Mary brought them down to her blazer and wiped off the oatmeal. I hadn't noticed until then, but she wore no rings on any of her fingers. For some reason, for a woman of her age, who could afford silk blouses, this seemed like some kind of statement, or position. I found myself wondering what her bedroom looked like, her bathroom, her vanity. She handed back the glasses and Dad stared at her through the clean lenses.

"So then," he said. "Next Friday?"

<hr/>

"You smell like cigarettes," he said in the truck after a few blocks. He said it calmly, factually, and didn't wait for my response but quickly supplied it: "It was her, I know. I saw the ashtray." He looked at me, as if I might confirm, or comment, or anything. But I could've been a crash test dummy. Until he coughed and said, "Seems a little unorthodox, is all," and I said, "It wasn't my idea to go in there," and that was the end of the cigarette discussion.

The truth was, I was thinking how great it would be to tell him that Mary Wintermantle used to date Michael Jordan—he wouldn't believe it!—but I wasn't ready not to be a little pissy yet that he'd forced me to see her in the first place.

"So what'd you talk about?" he asked at a stoplight.

"Dad," I said. "Confidential?"

"Right." He scratched his jaw. "Well, for her it is. But you could talk about it if you wanted to. I mean, if you wanted to talk to me about it, Jo—about whatever—you can, you know."

This was new—this trying to be a pal, to talk about *feelings*. He'd talked me to death about Roxanne, keeping me up nights while he waited to see if she'd come home. He talked to me as if I were the mother, and I went along with it, assuring him he'd not done anything terrible, that he was not a terrible father. And now I heard that voice again, that thin, unnerving night-voice, and it came to me that he was second-guessing the shrink decision, thinking maybe it was no different than changing school districts, that I would end up hating him for it and leaving him. A burst of feeling for him I couldn't understand or do anything with came into me, and so I just sat there, my heart pounding, until I saw he was going to run the red.

"Dad—*light?*"

He said "Shit" and hit the brakes and put his arm instinctively against my chest, then withdrew it quick.

"Listen," he said when the light turned green. The moment had passed; his regular dad-voice was back. "I need to stop at the Home Depot. Do you mind?"

Did I ever? Instead of one of the new, ready-to-go tract houses my classmates lived in, Dad had moved us into a "classic" on the far side of the district, a windy antique with dingy columns out front and narrow servant stairs in the rear, exactly the kind of old creaker Mom was always lusting after. There was not an inch of wall that did not need gutting and rewiring and rerocking, and Dad had gone head-first off the home improvement highdive. Before the move, he'd been a sports columnist for the *Trib*, but if he ever wrote anymore I never saw him do it. My room and his room and Roxanne's room and the kitchen and the living room were all finished, and now he'd moved on to the basement, turning it into something he called, in all seriousness, "the family room."

"For the life of me," he said as he drove, "I cannot find my twelve-inch mud knife," and then he gave me a look, a glance, as if my emergence as a liar might qualify me to explain where his tools were going all the time, when we both knew that the minute he bought a replacement, the old tool would turn up, usually while he was hunting for some other lost thing altogether.

Jack Bibby had given me the same loaded glance, I recalled with a chest-dive, before he asked me to recover his glasses.

———— ⤬ ————

"I could tell you about a dream," I said one afternoon.

It was the day before Halloween and in addition to the pizza and cigarette and scented candle smells, there were sugary spiderwebs of candycorn smell rising from a little pumpkin-shaped bowl on her desk. It was the only nod to the holiday, nothing else in the way of spooky décor, and after a long day at school it was good to see a grown woman without a fake wart on her nose.

"A dream?" Mary said.

"I mean I don't know if you're into that kind of thing or not," I said, and she stubbed out her cigarette and leaned forward and made a gesture like, *Please, begin,* and so I told her about this dream where I'd woken up in the middle of the night because someone had sat on the edge of my bed, and how I thought it was Dad but then I smelled the smoke and knew it was Rox. This was before she left home, this dream, so I wasn't all that shocked to see her.

"Did she often come into your room at night?"

"You mean in my dreams, or—?"

"I mean in real life."

"No. But in this dream, I wasn't surprised. It seemed very, you know, normal."

"OK. Go on."

"OK."

Are you awake? she said, and I said *I am now. What's going on? Nothing. I just wanted to come and bug you.*

Thanks a lot.

Shield your eyes, I'm gonna turn on this light.

Don't—

She clicked on my lamp and waited while I went through my convulsions.

Can you see now? she asked.

Yeah.

You sure?

Yeah.

What color are my eyes?

Black, like Satan's.

Har. Seriously, Jo, I wanna show you something. Can you see?

I can see, Rox, stop asking me that.

OK. I did this like a week ago, but I haven't shown anybody because it was still kinda gross, with the scabbing. But now it's ready and you're the first to see it, OK?

I didn't know what she was talking about. I was still half-asleep.

"In the dream," said Mary Wintermantle.

"What? Right. In the dream."

Roxanne shifted on the bed and unsnapped her jeans and hitched them down over her hip, thumbing down the black band of her underwear, her thong, and I suddenly knew what I was going to see—I mean I knew exactly. Even so, I gasped and flinched away when I saw it, as if the thing were alive, wildly buzzing up out of her jeans into my room.

It was a dragonfly. She'd always loved them, since before I was born. Mom kept an eye out for them at the crafts fairs and consignment boutiques: stocking-stuffer doodads sometimes and good jewelry other times, silver or white gold. Once, in the fourth grade, a kid brought a real one he'd pinned up on a black velvet pad, and at recess I snuck back in and stowed it behind some books—it needed to be with my *sister*, not some dumb kid! But the kid cried bloody murder and I pretended to find the specimen behind the books and everybody looked at me funny for a while, but whatever.

Mary was patient while I made my way back to the dream.

This dragonfly, though, on her hip...it had the look of realness and jewelry both. Nature and art both. The little body was inked in these deep blues and greens that played in the light like satin, and the four wings were these tiny see-through fans so realistic that I had the urge to run my fingertips lightly, lightly over them.

Go ahead, she said, *you can touch it.*

Dad's gonna kill you, I said.

Dad? she said. *How's Dad gonna know?*

I looked up, into her eyes, and she smiled, and I shivered, and looked down again at the dragonfly.

It's so lifelike, I whispered. *Did it hurt?*

Only if you don't like being stuck with a needle ten million times, she said. We were both of us looking at it, thinking our thoughts. Like we were waiting to see what it would do. When I touched it I almost screamed because it moved, it twitched—or her skin did, reacting to my finger. And it must've been right on top of a vein because after the twitch passed I could feel this little pulse, this little throb smaller than my fingertip.

It wasn't like anything I'd ever touched before. It was like touching something you weren't ever *supposed* to touch, like a famous painting, or a dead person, or your own heart. It made my heart pound, it made me almost sick with envy. *My* skin, the dragonfly said. *My* body. And I remembered thinking, later: if anything happened to her, anything terrible, any of those creepy TV things that were always happening to somebody's daughter somewhere, then the police would call and ask Dad if his daughter had a tattoo on her hip. Too bewildered to speak, he'd look at me, and I'd gently take the phone from him. "Describe it," I'd say calmly. "Describe this tattoo."

A small flame leapt up and I saw Mary Wintermantle before me.

She inhaled, then studied the smoldering tip of her cigarette at close range, then sidestreamed the smoke toward the open window and settled her eyes on me like moths.

"Are all your dreams like this, Josephine?" she asked, and I got the impression she would've liked to have smiled, maybe even giggled a little.

"Like what?" I asked.

"You know," she said. "So . . . lifelike?"

But it was I who giggled. And began to cry.

I continued to see her every Friday afternoon, on through Thanksgiving, and we continued to exchange sob stories (my mother had died in a terrible car accident! Her father was a drunk!), and Dad continued to pick me up even though I could have easily hopped the bus. Sometimes he and Mary would talk sports for a few minutes, and I watched him blush as he name-dropped the *Trib* on her—then saw him blush deeper when she said she knew it already, she'd read his columns religiously. I hadn't seen him interact with another adult woman like this since my mother, and I was surprised by how little it upset me.

One day, Dad and I came out of Mary's building and it was night already, and these big flakes like doilies were falling, and at the Home Depot they were selling Christmas trees, and so we picked one out and put it in the truck. But after we got home and hauled the tree in, and stood it in its stand, something just went out of us both, like ghosts, and we decided to wait for Saturday to trim it. Saturday came and neither of us mentioned the tree. Days and days went by and there it sat, a plain green conifer, dripping needles. Thanksgiving had been hard enough—the two of us at the Denny's, picking away at hot turkey sandwiches—and I didn't see how we'd ever get through Christmas. Our house had gone from three women to one, and I knew I wasn't much of one: I couldn't decorate a house or talk politics or tease him like Mom, I couldn't bring home trophies and make him laugh like Roxanne.

"Mmm," said Mary, as if she'd just bitten into a truffle. She tapped her cigarette and gazed at me gently but keenly: a look of steady, benign intensity. "It is the cosmic prank on all daughters, Josephine, to feel this way. At your age I was convinced that if I were smarter, or prettier, or funnier, or a boy, then Dad would not need to throw twelve bottles of beer down his throat every night." She inhaled, but forgot to exhale toward the window, and I watched a small cumulous rise over her head. Through this formation sailed Michael, her ex, leaping forever between her bookshelves. She leaned forward, close enough that I could see the mascara on her lashes. "But Jo, you and your dad are not doing so bad, all things considered. He may be a little obsessed with the house right now—but he's doing that for you, for the both of you. There is so much love in that!"

Was there? Could Sheetrock and paint and ceiling texture be the materials of love? Or were they the stuff you needed to repair the aftermath, the damage of love? Love was not this everyday home-improvement business—it was acts of drama and surprise and daring! It soared and crashed and vanished and devastated!

We were close, Mary and I, to a truth about me, about what I could and couldn't be to my father, about the relationship in my mind between love and trouble. And if I hadn't been in such a rush, if I hadn't been so terrified of a sad, quiet, civilized Christmas with Dad, we might have gotten our hands on it before I did what I did next.

But for now our time was up, and Dad was waiting.

———

I had one last session with Mary, the Friday before Christmas. She took longer than usual to emerge from her office and wave me in, so long that I almost fled. When she finally opened her door, I wished I had. She was ten years older. There was gray in her black roots, and bags like half-plums under her eyes. We took our seats and began to talk, but it was all flat, like we were reading from a textbook. And her eyes! For the first time since I'd known her, Mary's eyes drifted from my face—to the space above my head, to her cigarette ash, to the open window. It was almost a relief to have her look right at me—although, even then, looking her in the eye, I couldn't see anything but the blank space behind her, between the bookshelves.

Even Dad noticed when she opened the door to let me out.

"Where's Mike?" he said.

Mary shrugged and gave me an awful smile. "Left me again."

Did I mention the poster was signed? Do you know what a person could get for it on eBay? Even out of her school locker?

It took almost a week, but finally, searching for his speed square, Dad looked behind his tool chest and saw something stashed there, all but tossed there, like a roll of Christmas paper.

He found me in Roxanne's room, on her bed, turning her basketball in my hands. The ball smelled as if she'd played with it yesterday. Dampened the leather with her sweat, her hustle, the pure joy of her body. Dad sat beside me, the rolled-up poster in his fist. "What's going on here, Josephine?" The dread in his voice was all the more horrible for the upturn, at the end, of hope. "Did she give this to you?"

"No, Dad. I stole it."

"But—why? And how?!"

"I don't know why. And through the window she always keeps open. There's a fire escape out there. I went before school. I'm sorry, Dad."

And I was, truly. I had not prepared myself for how much I would hurt Mary, but I was even less prepared for how much I would hurt my father. I didn't know the difference between a daughter who lies, or smokes, or gets tattooed, or runs away, and one who is a thief. I heard a faint, papery winging sound and looked up from my twisting fingers.

But there was only him, staring at me through speckled lenses. "Jesus, Jesus," he muttered. "I thought you were getting *better*, Jo. You seemed almost happy!"

I had nothing for him but tears. I had done what I'd done. It was in his hands.

"You will take this back first thing tomorrow," he said.

"Okay," I sniffled. "I'll put it back before school."

"Like hell you will. You are going to hand it to her, Josephine. And apologize. Can you understand how devastated I am? How . . ." He looked away.

"Will you go with me?" I asked.

He made a snorting noise and shook his head. He smelled of latex paint. Little specks of it rode the hairs of his forearms like mites. "I feel like I stole this myself," he said.

"It's not like that, Dad. She's my *shrink*, for God's sake." I put my hand on his shoulder. "You think she doesn't know how messed up I am?" Touching him made me think of the last time we'd touched, which I remembered exactly because it was the night Roxanne walked out, and he had grabbed my arm as if he thought I might try to go, too. That was Christmas Eve, the year before. Her unopened gifts were in the room here, behind the closet door.

Dad didn't flinch at my touch. He didn't move.

"Was your shrink," was all he said.

—⁂—

We caught Mary on the street the next morning, dropping one of her brown cigarettes in the snow and sending it deep with her blue Uggs boot. She was looking better (*It fades*, I thought), and when she saw us her smile hit me in the throat, dislodging something large and burning.

"What on earth?" she said, taking the rolled-up poster from me. As she unrolled it, as Michael unfurled, soaring again, too many expressions crossed her face to keep track of, yet I knew I would remember each of them, exactly, the rest of my life. She unrolled until she saw the signature, then began rolling up again. By this time I was barely able to speak for the snot and the tears and the convulsions. Mary let me go on for a few seconds, then took me in her arms, pressing my flat chest against her full, deep, woman's one. I wanted to stay there. I wanted to die there.

A Kleenex appeared near my face. It smelled of her coat pocket, of her cigarettes and her hand lotion and her leather gloves. It smelled of good-bye.

She let go and reached for Dad, and hugged him too—just briefly, before coming back to thumb the tears from my face. She didn't want to hear another word about that poster! She wanted to buy us coffee in the café next to the pizza parlor.

Dad and I looked at each other and understood—he was right: Mary wasn't going to be my shrink anymore, not after this.

But she wasn't going to vanish, either. Some new arrangement was called for . . . we would have to figure out the terms.

Dad smiled, and nodded. But no, coffee wasn't possible, he had to get me to school. And he turned then to take my arm, or put his hand in the small of my back, or some other dad-like move, but all he got was air, for I was already at the curb, flailing my arms at the bus. If it didn't stop I would take off after it, flying down the sidewalk with everything I had, fast and light, like an athlete, like a dragonfly on the wing. Mary said she didn't want to talk about the poster but I knew she did, just not with me there. They both did. They had to. Theft is such a personal thing.

Antlerless Hunt

The young man had a truck in the air on a rotation job and he was in such a deep, thoughtless rhythm, nothing in his mind but the pneumatic burst of the driver, the clang of a lug in the pan, another scream of the gun, that it took a shout from the next bay over, half-deaf Haskins with that slug of plastic in his ear, to break him out of it. Haskins aiming an oily finger roofward, where the girl's voice was sounding again—the familiar amplified voice that was like a great girl-throated bird you never saw but which sang all day from the steel rafters, naming one man or another to come to the front desk, come sign something, come see her. Always some other man and never the young man, not in the six months he'd been at the shop, so that when he paused, and listened, and heard the girl say his name, all the blood seemed to pour from him like oil.

He drew a red rag from his pocket and walked head-down along the narrow aisle of other men's gazes, fixedly wiping at his fingers. His name was Tucker Russell. Ordinary-looking, of average height and weight, he was the youngest man at the shop, and certainly the oddest. Attempts to draw him out, to see what made him tick, to see what got his goat, had come to nothing. He was local-grown, as all of them were, and some of the men remembered him vaguely from when he had gone to high school with their sons. Or they remembered, when they learned his name, that he had played on the high school football team a few years back, that good team that almost won State; played, they remembered, but did not shine. They tried to remember if they'd seen his father at those games, or seen the man anywhere, ever, but they hadn't, and that seemed to say plenty.

Tucker entered the front room and was momentarily thrown by the failing light outside the big window, the beams of headlights plowing the dim street—it might've been a summer storm rolling in, only this was November, he remembered, the day after Thanksgiving; the sun had simply gone down, as it did in the winter.

At the sight of him the girl, whose name was Julie Sloan, rolled her brown eyes, but in a friendly way, for she was always friendly, even with the married men who hung on her counter joking and positioning for looks down her blouse. She was taking classes at the community college, and Tucker was taking classes too, as of that semester, though they were not the same classes or even the same fields of study; Julie Sloan was going to be a nurse; Tucker was going to teach high school English. He imagined sitting with her in the break room, their textbooks open, catching her eye from time to time, the little look she'd give him that said *We're not here forever, not us* . . . But each time he'd found her alone in the break room the air had emptied out of him, his heart had seized, and before he could recover, DeMarco or Kuntz had burst in calling, "Hey, don't mind us, you kids!" and come swooping over, buzzarding over her, improving their views down her blouse, "Whatcha reading, Jules? What's so fascinating, hey? let's have a look here . . ."

"*There* you are," Julie Sloan now said, and Tucker puffed out his cheeks like a man with great burdens, and went right for the phone. "Line two," Julie said, and then she got up and with a tug at her short skirt walked away toward the break room.

Tucker picked up the handset and pressed the blinking red button. "Hello?"

"Tucker?"

"Yes?" The handset was no ordinary handset: it lived in Julie's grip all day, against her ear, under a fragrant wing of hair. It touched her chin, her neck. It came this close to kissing her.

"Tucker goddam Russell—?"

Something kicked in Tucker's chest. Coldness touched the back of his head.

"You there? Tuck—?"

"Son of a bitch," Tucker said.

"I know," said the voice. It was Floyd Young. His old friend. "Some surprise, huh?" The cocky grin, the pale-blue eyes, snapped into place in Tucker's mind like pictures returned to their places on a wall. The grin that broke over Tucker's own face was the helpless grin of a child, or an idiot. He undid it, lowered his hand from the back of his head, and picked up Julie's pencil, with its Braille of small bite wounds. "Son of a bitch" he said again, then quickly added, "where are you?" and Floyd said, "Here, in town. Got back about a week ago."

"That right?" The pencil began digging into a notepad on the counter, a series of lines like prison bars, or the hash marks on a football field. "How'd you find me? I mean—"

"Old Doris, man," said Floyd. "She sounds just the same. Sweet as jam. Invited us to dinner in two seconds flat."

Us, Tucker caught, like an elbow.

"She did, huh?" he said. The pencil fractured on the paper, leaving a little bullet of lead lying there. He flicked it away and slipped the pencil into his pocket. "So how is old Kessler then?" he said. "She good, or . . . ?"

"Who?"

"Kessler."

"Oh. She's good. You know. Married life."

"Right," Tucker said. He could hear something in the background on the other end, a TV, or a radio tuned to a talk show.

He couldn't picture any kind of place but Floyd's family house on Pine Street, down the hill from the high school: the golden hardwood floors Floyd's father had laid and which his mother tried to keep from harm with every manner of rug.

"You didn't get hitched, did you?" Floyd asked. "Your mom didn't say."

"Me? Hell no."

"Smart man. What was I thinking, Tuck? We were goddam *kids*."

Tucker didn't answer, and Floyd went on: "Feels like a whole other life, doesn't it? All that high school bullshit?"

Julie came round the corner with a mug in her hands and there was a moment, an addled second, when Tucker didn't understand what she was doing there. At the same moment, Julie herself seemed to pull up, blink—something—at the sight of Tucker there, still there, at her desk.

"Listen, Floyd," Tucker said, "I got a truck up in the air—"

"Oh, hell yes, get back to work. I just wanted to check in with you, Tuck, you know. Let you know we were back and all."

"For good, then?" Tucker asked.

"For now," said Floyd. "Till we get our shit together. I'm working for the old man, laying floor. Meg's taking classes online. We can dump the kid off on the folks, and like that."

Julie came behind the counter with her mug. Someone had brought pie, and she'd sprayed a thick snowcap of whipped cream onto her coffee. She set down the mug and bent her knees and slipped a hand under her bottom with a soft little shhh. "There's a kid, huh?" Tucker said. There were towers of new tires in the room, and he could taste the bitter rubber on his tongue.

"Yeah, can you believe that? Me, a dad—?"

Tucker took a few steps away, as far as the twisted cord would allow. "Damn, Floyd. That's great." He heard his words down in the handset and only in the handset, as if they came from there, like a recording. "Congrats on that. Tell Kessler for me, OK?"

"Yeah," Floyd said flatly.

There was a silence. Julie sipped at her mug, then began tapping at her keyboard. There came the shrill report of a pneumatic driver, and somebody yelling something, and the chime of a dropped wrench, all of it loud inside the handset, inside both their ears.

"OK," Tucker said finally, and Floyd said, almost shouting, "Hey, before you go, Tuck—what're you up to Sunday?"

⸙

They had been friends a long time, almost as long as memory. Their mothers had both taught at the grade school, and it was this shared experience—the strangeness of watching your mother turn into Mrs. Russell, or Mrs. Young, giving her smile, her love, to other children—that first pushed them toward each other. Also, they discovered, they both could draw, and soon they were spending entire weekends at Mrs. Young's kitchen table, elbow to elbow, learning from the pages of comic books. They loved the same football team, Green Bay, and they loved the same knock-kneed girl, Jessica Owensby, although only Floyd had said so.

Tucker remembered the Wolfman.

He had brought to class one day a drawing of the Wolfman, frozen in mid-leap, great bristling arms flung out, jaws wide in outrage, in dismay as two silver bullets sizzled into his chest. Tucker slipped the drawing to a kid in math class and the kid passed it on and that was it.

No way he did that by hand, Jessica Owensby whispered. *You traced that,* an ugly girl said. The Wolfman reached Floyd, and Tucker's heart drummed. If he worked very long at a drawing, all but erasing the paper out from under him, he could produce something as good as what Floyd could do in ten minutes with hardly any erasing at all. A fact they both knew but never spoke of.

This is awesome, Floyd whispered at last.

He traced it, a boy hissed. *Nobody draws that good.*

Sure they do, Floyd said. *Watch.* And he flipped over his worksheet and got to work, looking from Tucker's drawing to his, scritching away. He never saw Mrs. Russell—Tucker's mother—coming, and after she'd snatched up the drawings, Floyd simply put down his pencil and waited. At her desk, Tucker's mother turned and seemed to haul the drawings up by their collars. *This*, she said, *is not what I mean by multiplication!* The class had only a moment, but it was enough. They went silent, heart-stopped, as if this second, unfinished Wolfman might crash, howling, into their desks. Tucker looked at the other kids, at Jessica Owensby, looking at Floyd, and he felt the same blackening spin he'd felt the time she'd caught him staring at her on the playground, and had smiled, and had called to him sweetly, *In your dreams, freakshow.*

The Wolfman was Tucker's last drawing. Before long, Floyd stopped drawing, too.

———

Sunday came. The alarm pulsing shrilly in the cold dark of Tucker's small apartment. He lay there wondering why it was going off, then got dully out of bed. Washed his face, shaved, combed his hair, made coffee, and sat at the little table watching the clock on the stove. The deer were killing crops and smashing cars and the state had added an early, antlerless hunt for the Thanksgiving weekend. Tucker had bought his license the day before, pulled his gun from the closet and cleaned the bore and oiled the barrel, thinking every few seconds, Call him back, tell him you can't do it, tell him no. You don't hear from the guy for two years—you don't *want* to hear from the guy—and now you're going out hunting with him, just like that?

He fixed a bowl of cereal but after one spoonful dumped it in the sink. It was four o'clock. He got into his boots, his jacket, his safety vest, his cap, and paused at the door for a glance around the little apartment, as if he would not be back, then carried his gun outside into the dark.

There was little traffic at that hour, a few 18-wheelers pounding east toward Chicago, the lakes, and west toward Denver and the mountains. He slipped in between them for the length of two exits and slipped out again, looping carefully around the frosty ramp and hitting the gas again under the overpass, heading south on Old Indian Highway. Crossing the river he looked down on a broken fog, shredded and lurking along the black surface like spirit canoes, and when he looked up again there was a deer—a big doe clambering up from the bank, onto the road. He heard the clatter of hooves as he hit the brakes and swerved, just finding the gap between the doe's hind quarters and the last iron reaches of the bridge. He straightened the car and saw the white flag of tail flick into darkness. Maybe one of them would kill her later, it crossed his mind.

They had learned guns together, too. Going out with Floyd's dad and older brother in the cold dawn, drinking cocoa from a Stanley, watching the morning seep like liquid through the trees, and with it, just as soundlessly, a pair of whitetails. Mr. Young held up his hand, then brought Floyd forward by the shoulder, put him in position for first shot—the only shot, it turned out, that day. But later, walking home, Mr. Young had put his hand on Tucker's shoulder, saying, "Next time, son," and Tucker had felt himself lift up into that hand, shivering, almost off the ground.

Floyd was first at everything. He'd grown stronger, faster, better-looking than Tucker, but somehow it didn't matter. When the high school coach cut Tucker from varsity, Floyd went in there and closed the door, and the next day Tucker was back on the line, throwing blocks for Floyd. Senior year they got jobs stacking lumber together and on their breaks Floyd talked about the cars they'd buy and the colleges they'd play for and the college girls they'd screw. He had it all figured out, for both of them.

———— ∞ ————

The house sat back from the county road, mailbox at a drunken tilt, Floyd's old Merc sitting in the drive like pure memory—the black, cracked bucket seats, the muscular rumbling, the green smell of spring rushing in and spring's first bugs popping on the windshield as Floyd gunned her down the highway.

The house was one of three faded houses caught between road and river, the middle child, and when Tucker pulled in behind the Merc the other two houses lit up with noise, the throats of multiple dogs disgorging a mad consensual alarm. He waited for a light to come on in the middle house—any house—for someone to shut up these dogs. If Floyd wasn't outside already waiting for him he was supposed to go on in. His foot was yet on the brake, the engine idling, his lights on the flaking paint scales of the house. No lights came on. He saw teeth behind the dark glass, the dagger fangs of some big breed, and that drawing came into his head again—the Wolfman. Leaping, outraged, dismayed.

He walked the gravel to the little wooden porch, and the dogs found a higher, more hysterical key. There was no bell to ring and he did not want to knock on the shabby door. So he did like Floyd told him and took the knob in his hand, and turned it, and with a sense of falling—of watching himself falling—he stepped inside.

Into dark and shadow and smell. Dark hulks of furniture and cardboard boxes, lightless windows on the far wall and a trapped, dense atmosphere of fried food and sour laundry. The absolute strangeness of someone else's home, their debris, their odors, rushing up over him like a foul water. He stood blinking in it, not breathing, listening. You'll have to make some noise, slam the door, call out . . . fifty barking dogs are not enough, the house has to be on fire, caving in, exploding—

"That you, Tuck?"

To his right, sleepy, thick, a girl's voice. He could see the crown of her head, the light frizz of hair against the pale wall. "That you, Kess?" he said. Something was wrong with the floor: he took a step for balance.

"Shh," she said. "Got the boy here."

"You do?" he said in a ragged whisper. "Floyd said you had one."

"He was right. Come see."

The dawn was coming, or his eyes were adjusting, but now he could see her, seated in a wooden rocker with a small child piled up against her. The child wore a thick pajama but she was in a loose gown. Long pale legs crossed at the ankles. He stepped on something small that gave with a click like a mine and he stopped.

"Dang," he said.

"It's nothing. Come on," she said.

He went on, he went up to her, the milky smell of the baby and the heat of their bodies rising to meet him. Her gown was open at the collar and the bones there looked like young antlers under the skin. He saw her smiling the same smile, those big eyes, the face a little puffed from lack of sleep, or crying, or being a mother.

Meagan Kessler, said his heart. *My god.*

She leaned forward to show him the child and Tucker's eyes briefly fell down the front of her robe—the pale swell of breast, the dark rose of areola.

He gazed intently at the child, the meaningless little face and said: "He looks good, Kess. He's a good-looking boy."

"You think so?" She regarded the child, then looked up and regarded Tucker the same way. Her eyes gathered wet light from somewhere, and with an unsteady smile she said, "Damn, Tuck. What's a girl gotta do to get a kiss around here?"

He stared at her. He wasn't sure he'd heard her correctly. His heart rolled on a sea wave, and in the next moment from behind him a voice said: "What's going on here?" and he turned to see a shirtless, pallid, soft-looking Floyd Young coming at him. Tucker didn't move. He stood there. He had wondered what he would do if he ever saw Floyd Young again, and now he knew: he would do nothing.

Floyd came on, the old grin breaking loose, his great arms flung out, then flung around Tucker in a fleshy, sour-smelling clench. "God damn, look at you," Floyd said, standing back again. "You look just the same. Like somebody put you in a vault. Don't he, Meg?" Floyd stood in his boxers grinning. He slapped his hands to his wobbling gut. "I stopped playing ball and now I'm having a goddam baby."

Meagan said from her rocker, "If there's a baby in there he's shaped like a can of beer," and Floyd snorted and said, "He sure ain't shaped like a good meal, I know that much," and Meagan said, "Oh, that's good, Floyd, that's pure class," and Floyd said, "You started it," and in the long look she gave him Tucker heard everything else she wanted to say, and had said, and would say when they were alone again.

Floyd turned to Tucker: "Gimme two shakes, OK?" Then, over his shoulder as he returned to the bedroom: "Why don'tcha put a light on so he can see it?" and Meagan replied, "Great, and when he wakes up you can get him back to sleep."

Tucker stood there. Now he saw the plastic toys on the floor, the dirty plates on the coffee table. He saw two tiny moons of light and looked closely. A black cat, watching him from the basin of a black, buckled sofa. The sound of Floyd pissing ended the silence, his stream plunging heavy and long into the water; clearing his throat like an old man, hocking it into the bowl; flushing everything down. Was that Mr. Wiggly, her old cat? Tucker asked, but it wasn't, Mr. Wiggly had been run over by a car.

Tucker stood there. The child reached up in sleep to punch at Meagan's breast. "How's your mom, Tuck?" she asked. "Gosh I always liked her," but before he could answer, here was Floyd again, shuddering the floor with his boots. He smacked Tucker on his way to the door. Tucker said, "See ya, Kess," but she held him there with her eyes. They could hear Floyd's boots cracking the cold wooden steps outside.

"Call me sometime, Tuck," Meagan said. "OK?"

———

Floyd gave a whistle at the Ford in the drive, running his hand along the fender—was it new?

Tucker was drawing the cold deeply into his lungs. The dogs had quit wailing and didn't seem to care that he and Floyd were out here crushing gravel under their boots. It wasn't new, hell no, but the lady before didn't drive much. Still, Floyd said, ducking in, it looked new. Even *smelled* new. Tucker pulled onto the highway, leaving the house and the Merc and the girl and the child behind in the dark.

Floyd twisted for a look at the back seat. "Still got that Rem, I see," he said.

"That still your dad's?" Tucker said.

"Yeah. Though I guess it's safe to say it's mine, though, after all these years."

They drove over the river, then up onto the interstate, then off again for coffee from the Gas-N-Go. Floyd pretended to hold the glass door for Tucker but at the last second cut in ahead of him—an old gag. He clomped around, whistling. He slapped a copy of JUGS to Tucker's chest and Tucker put it back. When they got to the counter the man nodded at Tucker's vest and asked where they were headed and Floyd said, "We could tell ya, but then we'd have to kill ya," and the man looked at Floyd, smiled crookedly and said, "Don't tell me, then." They were back on the road, traveling west on the 41 before Tucker looked over and said, "Where's your orange?"

Floyd was stabbing at the presets on the radio, his cheek swollen with doughnut. "Bottoma some box," he said, and a birdshot of white paste appeared on the dash. "Shit, sorry," he said, wiping at it, smearing it.

"You gotta have something, Floyd," Tucker said, surprised by his anger. *Dumbshit*, he thought. *Fatass*. "You can't go like that. Here, take this."

"I don't want your fuckin hat. Ain't nobody gonna be out there but us anyway, fuck's sake."

The highway intersected the interstate, and as they drove under the bridge they both looked to the right, to the concrete bank that rose steeply from the shoulder up to the dark iron girders, and they both thought the same thing: *Kurt Spitzer*.

It was two bridges, in fact, one for each direction, with a gap of several feet between the low barrier walls. Kurt Spitzer had been a senior when Tucker and Floyd were ninth-graders, a fact that compelled the weed-reeking Spitzer to toss both boys, on separate occasions, into the cafeteria Dumpster. Welcome to high school. Later that autumn, Spitzer and a guy nobody knew, some drop-out friend of his from another district, were walking along the interstate at two a.m. They'd run out of gas, and they'd been drinking but not fighting, this other boy later told police. They'd walked for miles, trying to get back to the gas station. At some point, they decided to cross the interstate, and Spitzer vaulted himself over the concrete divider and disappeared. They were on the bridge. They didn't know about the gap, the other boy said.

Not long after the memorial assembly at school, where a girl with inky tears read her terrible poem, Floyd and Tucker rode bikes out to the overpass. The talk at school was Foul Play: both boys had been in love with the girl with the inky tears, and the other boy, Spitzer's friend, had planned the whole thing out of jealousy.

Under the overpass Floyd and Tucker expected, and searched for, among the good-bye graffiti and the litter of flowers and cards, some mark yet on the concrete, a stain perhaps yet tacky where the boy had lain with the blood leaking out of him, but they couldn't find it. They sat in the shadowed cool under the steel spanners looking down on the upside-down messages chalked onto the concrete, arms wrapped round their knees while the semis thundered overhead and roared on, east, west, having no idea. They had known this boy, had seen him walking and talking; had felt his muscles and smelled his breath when he got them into a headlock. This boy, this teenager, who had experienced things far beyond their own experience, such undiscovered things as sex and betrayal and jealousy, and death.

Driving under the bridges, Tucker looked up and remembered sitting there with Floyd. He remembered that he had wanted to say something, to tell Floyd something (what was it?), but that the chill and thundering silence of the place, the bewildered ghost of the dead boy, had kept him from speaking.

"Kurt fucking Spitzer," Floyd said, in the car. "Do you remember that douche-bag?"

———

They parked in front of the old cattle gate with the NO TRESPASSING sign, got out and opened the gate and walked into the woods. Old Man Saunders was friends with Floyd's dad from the house-building trade and it was here on this land that Floyd and Tucker had learned to shoot years ago, going out early with Mr. Young. It was OK with Saunders if the boys did their hunt here, so long as they kept well clear of the house.

The sun was not yet up but there was light to see by and they walked single file, barrels down and both falling automatically into silence. They came to a grassy pasture and began to work their way around it from just inside the tree line. The yellowing grass was pressed and spiraled where a herd had slept. It looked to Tucker like the place where Floyd had shot his first deer, that first time out, when Floyd's dad had handed him the gun, saying, *The heart, Floyd. Don't forget.* But the woods were full of places that looked like this, and nothing you remembered as a kid could be trusted anyway.

They walked around the pasture and kept going, deeper into the land. They heard no other hunters, no faint pop of rifles, only their steps and the waking birds and their own breath in their ears. After a period of dense trees they came to another clearing, this one paling in the sun's first rays, and they again made their way around, keeping to the tree line. At some point he didn't notice, Tucker began to feel a sense of clarity. As if the curtain of some long-dulling illness were lifting, peeling the world bare. Up in the branches in the new light he saw the curled shells of leaves twisting red and yellow on their stems. He heard beetles dragging their bellies through the forest litter. He smelled the coming freeze in the pine pitch and in the bright moss on the trunks.

Floyd looked back with a smile, and Tucker gave him a nod. The rifle cradled in his arm seemed an object of perfect balance and fineness.

Floyd stopped abruptly, and Tucker stopped. They listened. A crow threw down an irritated croak. Leaves on the branches dryly bristled. As if to investigate some potential danger, Floyd signaled Tucker to stay put, and went on alone. Tucker didn't expect him to move the way he used to, but he did, with the same surprising light-footedness, slowed here for stealth, with which he'd once confounded tacklers. When he was fifty yards ahead he stopped and took a knee, and aimed his barrel through a sparse fence of cover into another clearing: two deer out there. A doe and a young, antlerless buck. Both fair game—yet Floyd had signaled Tucker to wait, to hold back. Nothing else would've occurred to him, Tucker understood—or to himself. It had been established years ago and never changed: Floyd would go first.

Floyd ungloved his hand with his teeth. He thumbed off the safety.

Gotta tell you something, Tuck.

A warm, sweet night in May, a school night, just before graduation—driving that Merc around. Muscled arms out the windows, drinking PBRs and cruising the college, around and around, as if it was already theirs. For once in his life Tucker was feeling equal, like he could hold his own with Floyd Young. It was because of Meagan Kessler. She had broken up with her boyfriend of two years and the pack was closing fast, but Tucker saw her one day sagged against her steering wheel, and he pulled over in his new, used GMC. Walked up to her window and said, Need a jump?

The girl lifted her face. Blue eyes under water but a look like she might burst out laughing. Are you serious?

I got good cables, Tucker said, and she did laugh—a great wet sob of a laugh.

We had A.P. together, first trimester, he said. Ms. Tanzini.

I know. Meagan drew her hand under her nose with a raucous sniff. She read like five of your papers, she said. We all hated you.

Tucker scratched his jaw and looked up the street.

But you never said boo all tri, Meagan said. She said this as if it were a concern of hers, as if it were something she'd puzzled over. He looked into her car, squinting diagnostically at her gauges. Hmm, he said—and the door-ajar light flashed on, and the opening door swung into him. She was shimmying over to the passenger seat. Come on, she said, you can do better than that.

They ate burgers, and later they sat on her back porch in the dark listening to the coming thunderstorm. Veins of lightning throbbing the world. With the first big notes of rain on the tin roof, she tapped him on the shoulder. Why don't you come here and kiss me? she said. It was a long kiss, the longest ever. His hand on her throat, on the thudding soft rope of jugular, and her hand on his hand there, a weight that helped draw it down, over those collar bones and down, down into the V of her blouse. A button gave way as if it were nothing and her cool breast filled his hand. *Boo*, he said suddenly, into her ear, and she laughed, and her breast seemed to laugh in his hand.

He had just happened by, but that had been enough. She had picked him. And the word went out: Russell and Kessler.

Gotta tell you something, Tuck, Floyd said, in the Merc.

They were back in the car, in the stadium parking lot. They'd just returned from a piss in the shadows, under the starblown sky, and Tucker was wondering if she was still up. He had this idea of going by her house and hitting her window with a pebble. She'd meet him on the porch, in her robe.

Floyd was talking. He said Meagan's name. Stars began to burn across the sky, streaking every which way in a sudden and insane reordering. The sound of it, a raw stellar wind, roared inside the car. The two of them were changing, too—he and Floyd, morphing as they sat there into entirely different men, with no shared past, no shared memories, all of it pouring out of the car like water. It was too much to understand, to feel, and he thought his life must be about to end, that this must be what it feels like when the silver bullet goes in, when the skull finds the pavement.

It was just something that happened, Tuck.

He got out of the Merc and began walking. *Tuck, come on . . . Don't be a pussy about this.* Tucker wanted to say something back, something so hard and cold neither of them would ever forget it, but it took all his concentration just to make his legs move.

Meagan tried to call him. She left messages with his mother, and then she stopped. Floyd came by the house, but was likewise intercepted and parentally turned away. At graduation Tucker watched Meagan Kessler cross the stage, then he crossed it himself, and then immediately left the auditorium. A few weeks later, Floyd and Meagan were gone. In the days and weeks to follow, in the hot empty days of summer, Tucker's anger and humiliation gave way to a heartsickness which he gradually understood had more to do with Floyd than Meagan. This boy whom he'd known almost all his life like a brother, like a twin. The absence was too sudden, too absolute. He walked around with a strange feeling of weightlessness, as if at any second he might rise irretrievably into the air.

A crow was calling down from the sky. Sunlight scrolled along the black of his barrel, and he squinted through it. All that was two years ago. More than two years. Tucker had not kissed another girl since. Across the clearing, beyond Floyd, the doe put her glassy walnut eye right on him. The fur on her throat stirred in the wind, and Kurt Spitzer fell again into Tucker's mind—vaulting over that divider and finding nothing to land on but darkness. It wasn't foul play, he knew. It was just an accident. Two boys out by themselves, walking. Any stupid thing could happen.

The small buck stepped idly in front of the doe, exposing himself broadside to the clearing, and Tucker pulled the trigger. The stock punched his shoulder and both animals flinched as the round split the air between them, and an instant later they wheeled and flew away, like the sound of the shot, into the trees.

Floyd lowered his gun and thumbed the safety back on. He came back, moving loud and careless as any man anywhere, out for a stroll. The crow was gone and the wind had died. He stood beside Tucker and stared through the trees to where the deer had been. He stood close to Tucker. Anyone watching would've thought they were talking low, calling a play. In time Floyd did speak, he said Tucker's name, and Tucker turned and began to walk back to the car.

At Floyd's house he left the engine running. The sun was up and every dent in the old Merc was visible, every gray curl of paint on the little house. No dog barked, and he wondered if he'd imagined that earlier, if the mind could do something like that.

Floyd made no move to get out but only sat there, staring out, crushing one big hand in the other. He was about to say something when Tucker spoke up—asking if he remembered the Wolfman . . . ? That drawing he'd done in grade school, of the Wolfman?

Floyd's eyes came round to him. "What?"

"The Wolfman," Tucker said. "That drawing everybody said I traced."

Floyd looked away.

"But you stuck up for me," Tucker said. "Remember?"

Floyd gave a kind of huff. He shook his head. "Christ, Tuck."

"Even though you knew I traced it," Tucker said. "Didn't you," he said.

Floyd gave him his pale blue eyes to look into. Then he looked at the gun between his knees, the dark deep tunnel of the barrel. "So?" he said flatly. "We were friends."

Tucker nodded.

"I just wondered," he said. "All these years I just wondered if you knew, that's all."

Floyd looked up again. He looked out the window at the bright November morning and the stark little house he would soon go into. There was a sudden noise in the air, the urgent banter of geese, and a moment later the big necky birds came beating into view, low over the water, a broken chevron chasing its dull image down the gray river south. The two young men watched the birds go.

Tucker was surprised to find Julie Sloan in his mind—the girl from work. Her smile, the sound of her voice filling the shop, the way she tucked her hair behind her ears when she studied. The idea that Floyd knew nothing about her—nothing at all about this new life of his—at first made him want to smile. But in the next moment he understood that it would not amount to anything, ever, if he didn't tell Floyd. He would go on working at the shop and never speak to her and one day she would not be there, having quit to begin her life as a nurse, and he would not see her again until the day a tire exploded in his face or the lift gave out and by then it would be too late, she'd be dating the young doctor who was stitching him up, because she was beautiful and smart and any doctor, married or otherwise, could not help wanting her.

Tell him, Tucker thought. Tell him, and then Monday morning you can talk to her. You can bring her a cup of coffee and ask her about school, about nursing, and after that everything will be different. DeMarco, Kuntz, Haskins, they'll stop laughing behind your back and they'll stop trying to cop looks down her blouse and they'll shut up when the two of you are trying to study because they'll know, they'll finally know, and there won't be a thing they can do about it but wish it was them instead of you.

While all of this was pulsing through his brain he didn't notice Floyd staring blankly out the windshield—blankly but intensely, as if following some raw, dismaying narrative of his own. And when he did look over and saw his friend's face, it gave him a sickly, plummeting feeling, as if he'd looked into a dizzy gorge. It was this moment he would remember, some years later, when he walked into the break room and saw the men staring at the TV; Floyd had been out on the river behind his house, testing the ice before letting his boy skate out, and had fallen through and been swept away. *I remember that kid*, DeMarco would say. *Ran the ball like a goddam panther. Hell*, Haskins would add, *I thought he ran right outta this town years ago.*

"You know what I wonder about?" Floyd now said, in the car, his voice as strange and remote as his eyes. "Kurt Spitzer. Jumping over that divider. That second when he went over and there was nothing there and he was just, falling." Floyd blinked, and for a moment he seemed to see what was actually before him: the gray little house, the flat gray river beyond. "I keep thinking: in that second, in that instant, Tuck, in the dark—did he know?"

Jumping Man

A child goes missing one afternoon, somebody's little girl, and the news is a stick, an accurate rock, to the quiet hive of Sunday. Mowers are killed mid-lawn, propane grills are snuffed, wet limbs are plucked from pools and sorted and banished from water, from fun itself, until further notice. Adults and teenagers fan out, lacing the air with the missing girl's name like the call-and-answer of a whole new game: *jay-nee . . . jay-nee . . . jay-nee!*

We all have cell phones, we all know the number to call when we find her, we all secretly believe we will be the one to make the call—to tell her mother that Janie is fine, not kidnapped or molested, simply lost on her bike in the vast clone job of lawns and houses. And who hasn't been? Pulling our cars into the wrong drive, wondering whose big dog is chained to our tree, where the rose bushes came from. It's our inside joke—What a beautiful house!—and when somebody else's kid walks big-eyed through the front door we are kind, we are patient, we don't send her out again until we know where she belongs.

We search through the dusk for Janie Wilson, then through the twilight, until it becomes difficult to make out faces on the opposite side of the street. Is that Dr. Kidman, the foot surgeon, walking in flip-flops? Is that Aaron Dorfman of the Seven Dwarfmans, which wild brood will leave your pool four inches low every time? Their voices aren't helpful, somehow; out here in the quickening dark, calling the name of a child who is not our own, we all sound alike.

At least I hope we do. I mean my own voice to sound urgent but not desperate; as intense, but not more so, as the next man's. I wonder if I'm succeeding, or if everybody who hears me knows exactly who I am.

When I hear another man up ahead on the sidewalk, I stop calling, because this voice I recognize and I know he'll recognize mine. But silence is not an option, not tonight, so I resume calling "jay-nee!" and Jeff Finney answers "jay-nee!" in his deeper register, until we can see each other clearly, until our voices collide overhead like pterodactyls.

Here's the situation: Jeff has covered his territory and I have covered mine; we should stop and walk back to the Wilson house together, try to figure this out like men. Instead he slides me a glance—the most indifferent, most *contumelious* I've ever seen from a grown man—and continues on. "Jay-nee!"

I keep going too, but as I move into the space he's just vacated I falter, I spasm like a sleepwalker waking up—everything is familiar and wrong at once, an upending wave of déjà vu. Out of it comes a name—

Miranda Hessy

—and in the next instant I'm shocked in the ears by a shrill, mini alarm.

It's my cell phone. They're lighting up all over, like fireflies. I answer with hope, but the news isn't good: the police are packing it up for tonight, my wife tells me. Olly olly oxen free. Phones stop ringing and voices stop calling and the neighborhood goes so quiet, so suddenly graveyard, not even the dogs know what to do.

Carmen Wilson stands in her driveway with a circle of women around her, all touching some part of her—shoulders, hands, her inky long hair. There's a police officer in there as well, also female, and she has the floor. Beyond that is a wider circle of adults who look on but do not try to butt in or listen too closely; they are the human Do-Not-Cross line that keeps the rest of us, the remaining adults and teenagers, well away from whatever the officer is telling Carmen Wilson to do with herself now. I'm part of this outer outer ring and so is Jeff Finney, and I can see by the grind of his jaw that he wishes he was farther out still. It's the cops; he still thinks they're out to screw him. In fact they came pounding on his door earlier in the summer. Until that night, Jeff had enjoyed a unique standing in the neighborhood, as it was his company that contracted these houses, and if they are not very imaginative houses at least they are well-built: your noise doesn't spill into your neighbor's bedroom unless you both have your windows open, and that's what happened to Jeff.

He went down a few pegs after the D & D call, and a few more after Stacey moved out, but I tried not to judge. Jeff had had a tough childhood, I reminded myself. We'd gone to grade school together, plus one year of junior high, on the far side of town, the old side where the houses can be any shape or size. Jeff's dad was not altogether right in the head. The way you knew this was not because he'd been in Vietnam, but because when he got a few Hamm's beers in him he would grab you and hold you until you cried "God bless America!" Jeff's mom wore a hairnet in the cafeteria at the junior high and had bad hearing like an elderly person. They'd had another son, years older than Jeff, who, Jeff said, had been killed in a high-speed chase. His name was Ryan, and the door to his room stayed shut.

The Finney house was small but it was a good place to stop after school because there were always school-made cookies in the kitchen, and it became a game (more to me maybe than to Jeff) to get in there and grab some without having to say "God bless America!" Some days, I was abruptly sent home and I could hear the yelling from the street. Other times, Jeff just showed up at my house nine blocks away. I had a big house, and he liked all the places we could go without seeing a single other person.

That old man had his moments, though. One day out of the blue he brought home a puppy. Jeff named him Jimbo and we rushed to his house every day after school to play with him, and to take turns running him on the leash. Before long, Jimbo became a powerful big dog who could destroy any toy with his teeth. He got so big neither one of us could pick him all the way up, and he ran us off of our feet, he pulled our shoulders from our sockets.

One afternoon, as we were leaving the garage for the first run, Jimbo lunged before Jeff was ready, and Jeff jerked back hard on the leash, and Jimbo gave a strangled howl. That should've been the end of it, but Jeff drew back his hand and whacked the dog on the ass, and the dog spun around and attacked. "Get him off, get him off!" Jeff was crying, and after a stunned moment I grabbed Jimbo's collar and leaned back until his front paws were up in the air, dog-paddling. He kept snapping his teeth, but I wasn't afraid. In fact part of me was thrilled: Jimbo wanted to kill Jeff—oh boy did he—but he was letting me stop him.

From a distance, Jeff raised his hand and I saw the deep puncture in his palm before it filled with blood and the blood spilled down his arm.

The next morning he came by my locker with his bandaged hand. "Don't tell anybody about this," he said in a strange, flat voice. "You do, you'll never see him again." He meant Jimbo, and a lot more, and though I didn't much like him at that moment, I knew I'd never tell anybody how I'd saved his ass from his own dog—and that this, somehow, was even more heroic.

I caught up with him after school and we walked to his house in a hard silence. His dad met us at the door and told me to go on home, then took Jeff inside. He'd never looked so sane and sober, that old man. He'd had Jimbo put to sleep while we were at school.

It was a shock to see Jeff Finney again all these years later, living in one of these houses. I recognized him at once and I know he recognized me, but we faked it for as long as we could, until we found ourselves trapped at a barbeque, Michelobs in hand, and gave up. We didn't become friends again, but we got friendly enough that I was a day or two from taking on his divorce when I heard from Karen Dorfman that he was having *a thing* with Carmen Wilson, whose own art-dealer husband had left her a few months before for his leggy assistant and a year in Prague. I was already handling Carmen's divorce, and I was appalled. I blindly grabbed some folders and walked to her house in the middle of the day. She stood in the doorway and told me Jeff had been talking about me. About what a weird one I'd been as a kid.

"Excuse me?" I said.

"Those magazines?" Carmen replied. "What you said you wanted to do to those women—?" She crossed her arms at the abdomen.

"What?" I put a hand on her doorjamb to steady myself and she quickly uncrossed her arms. "Carmen—what did he say?"

"If you think I'm going to repeat it—"

My neck was pounding. "Carmen, Jeff Finney is a *liar*. Did he tell you about his dad? Did he tell you that story?"

She narrowed her eyes and waited—but I couldn't do it. The lawyer in me, or maybe the friend I'd once been to Jeff, couldn't tell her.

"I never had any magazines!" was all I could say, in a voice I hadn't heard since puberty. "They were *his*."

It was enough. She didn't speak to me for two weeks. But she didn't speak to Jeff Finney either, and for that, and maybe much more than that, he gut-punched me in broad daylight. One good one that dropped me to my knees. Everybody saw it. Amy saw it. My boy saw it. A mess.

Jeff Finney had always been good with his hands.

My chat with Carmen reminded me of the little room he'd built in the rafters of his garage, using plywood we'd poached from a house down the street that was under repair. The room wasn't much bigger than a dog house, but Jeff had laid in for the long term: packing blankets, Winston 100's, Cheetos, a huge, coplike flashlight, and a magazine he said he'd found in Ryan's bedroom. I'd seen the covers of such magazines before—out of reach behind drugstore counters but cruelly, openly studied by men in barbershop chairs—and it was all I could do not to rip this one from his hands as he casually riffled the pages. At last he stopped, stared for a long moment, exhaled a smoky *woof*, and dropped the magazine in my lap. A full-page woman, on her back, gazed up at me. There was a man, too, but all you could see of him was his penis, which she held to her mouth like a microphone. Her breasts were pale globes shined up with goo, and her legs were spread and with her other hand she was pushing something, a white, tusklike object, into her vagina, which looked sore.

Jeff loomed forward with the flashlight and when he did I was jolted by the effect—by how much larger he suddenly was, and older. I could smell his body, his underarms, the grease of his hair, and when he spoke, souring the air with Cheetos breath, I heard the voice of his dead brother. The little room pitched, my stomach convulsed, and I puked into a packing blanket.

It was the cigarettes, we concluded: I was a lightweight and had smoked too fast. He made me drop the blanket through the trap door and take it with me. I was sick all the way home, and each time I wretched I smelled his Cheetos breath and I saw the sore vagina, and I hated him for building that room in the rafters. Somehow, he had changed his whole house.

This was not long after Jimbo was put to sleep, and not long before Miranda Hessy went missing.

By the end of the second day, Janie Wilson's face is all over town, an Amber Alert is in effect, and we are all so tired. It's a relief to come back home and to feel—*relief.* To know that we are home and that our own children are safe. It's a reason for Amy to make the chicken Alfredo I love and to stir up brownie mix for later (what is more reassuring, more settling, than the business of dinner in your own home?), and for the kids to turn off the TV at first call and for us all to hold hands while Lilly gives thanks and asks God to please please take care of Janie Wilson because, as God already knows, Janie is her best friend.

It doesn't solve our problems, this terrible development—Amy's hand is still a tense little fish in mine—but it does seem to drain some of the water from our lungs; there's air for breathing again, even for talking. Daniel gets us going.

"Dad, can I ask you something?" At twelve he's growing special sensors; he's concerned about protocol, about the etiquette of families who are not missing children. But he is also more careful in general, I have noticed, more . . . calculating. He organizes leaves of spinach on his plate.

"Of course," I say.

"You know *Popeye*, the cartoon?"

"They still show that?"

"On the Cartoon Channel, sometimes."

"Man, I loved Popeye. '*I yam what I yam and that's all—*'"

"Yeah," he says quickly, "that's him. But you know how Popeye and Bluto are always kicking each other's ass?"

"Daniel," Amy says.

"I heard that," says Lilly. "I heard 'ass.'"

"Eat, young lady."

"Yes," I tell my son. "Bluto always kicked Popeye's keister until you-know-what."

Dan wags a leaf of spinach and makes the face a son must make to such a dad.

"Your question?" I ask.

"My question is they fight, like, all the time, right? And every time it's over Olive Oyl, right? Bluto grabs her, and then Popeye has to get her back, and that's the whole thing—right?"

My heart is suddenly thudding. I don't dare look away from him. "Pretty much," I say. "He has to get her back, and he does."

"Exactly," he says, and I recognize the satisfaction, the *pleasure*, in his tone—I have heard it, I have used it, many times in court. "But the thing is—" Dan pauses. He wants the whole room's attention. "The thing is, Dad: Olive Oyl's a *skank*."

"Danny!" Amy yelps.

"What? She is! She *wants* Bluto to grab her. And not only that, but has anybody, like, *looked* at her—?"

"What's a skank?"

"Never mind!"

"But what is it though? What is it, Danny?"

"It means she's a—"

"Daniel Joseph—"

"What? Am I wrong? I mean am I missing something? Dad—?"

We've gone so far beyond protocol there's no way for me to respond. I can't agree—I'm not even certain my son knows what he's saying—and I certainly can't laugh. All I can do is stuff Alfredo into my mouth until there's no way to tell what I think.

"Whatever she is," Amy says, fixing her eyes on him, "whatever you may think of Olive Oyl, it does not amuse or please me to hear you describe anyone that way."

"Mom: she's not even real."

"Language is real, Danny! Words are real. OK? And what I hear is the language of a little jerk, and that is the last thing I want to hear out of my own son's mouth."

The boy is stunned. We all are.

"Do you understand what I'm saying?" she adds in a milder tone, trying to pull back—but too late: a portcullis has slammed down over his face. He gets so angry, so fast! He sets down his fork and stares straight ahead as if he sees something in the window. As if Janie Wilson is there, looking in, wondering who these red-faced people are in her house.

⸙

Amy is upstairs a long time with Lilly, a major Monday-night bathing event while I clear the table and load the dishwasher and bake the brownies and walk the floor. There is cunning in how long she's up there, a knowledge of the fact that however long she takes, it can never be thrown back at her as an act of aggression: she is *bathing our daughter.*

From the window over the sink I can just see Carmen Wilson's front lawn. An oblong of light lies on the cut grass like a doorway to a cellar. I watch this light for several minutes, until—there: it pulses once, then again, as bodies pass through her living room. I lift my eyes to the upper floor, braced for light in a window, but there is none, and there is none, and the oven alarm goes off and I jump, I flail, bee-stung from the sink.

Daniel won't come down for brownies so I take one up to him. He's at his desk digging his pencil into a drawing pad. He and David Dwarfman have been making comic books. They each have their own rosters of Good and Evil, duly battling, but the real contest, I think, is between the two boys. David is the superior artist, I admit, but Daniel has better characters. My favorite is Jumping Man. Jumping Man didn't know he had superpowers until he jumped from the burning WTC—*and walked away.* Nobody noticed in all the mayhem, and now he's jumping, and kicking ass, for the U.S. of A.

"Brought you a brownie," I say.

"Thanks," he says without looking up.

Dan's happy to show his drawings when he's done but he doesn't like to be watched, so I set the plate on his desk and go to his window. It's the same view as from the kitchen, I note, only better, more comprehensive—and it grabs at me suddenly, pulls me into a sickly vertigo.

I have mainly kept my head about Carmen Wilson. I have mainly waited for the exigencies of lawyering for my chances to be alone with her, and yet—. There were one or two nights, possibly as many as three, when I stole out of the house while my family slept, my veins pounding with the idea that she was up—that she would meet me in her back yard, by the pool. Would let me sink my hands into her hair again, bind them in damp black ropes, the clean scent rising with the grass and the night jasmine and the chlorine as she took me into her mouth again. It was such a consuming, mad vision that I never gave a thought to this window—to my son, standing in the dark watching me, his father, mincing down the street in a hideous cartoon tip-toe. He might've known about Carmen Wilson long before Jeff Finney punched me in the stomach.

The thought fills me now with such shame I want to throw myself out my son's window—I want to become Jumping Man!

At the very least I know I should turn around and talk to him, tell him how sorry I am, what a disaster I know I am.

There he is, hunched over his desk. The bony little shoulders. The scritch scritch of his pencil. "New comic?" I say, and he mechanically answers, "No."

"Jumping man?" I press.

"Jumping man's dead," he says, and true shock rolls through me. It flips my heart.

"What? How?"

Those shoulders give an irritated jerk. "He lost his powers. He went splat."

I stand there a long time, too long, watching the boy. The hard, concentrated silence of him. Whatever I had to say to him is gone.

At the door, I turn back.

"By the way—about Olive Oyl?" I say. "She's trouble, I agree. But not a skank."

Those shoulders shrug once more. "It's a cartoon, Dad."

There is nothing skanky about Carmen Wilson, let the record show, Jeff Finney notwithstanding. On the other hand, if you want to know what's so great about her, what compelled me to drive such pain into my wife's heart, to risk the loss of my children, I'm going to let you down. I don't know the answer to that one. Maybe only that she had been wounded and seemed to need me. Though, in retrospect, I wonder if I was merely handy, which is as sad as it gets.

No, this is sadder: it doesn't change a thing. I still want her! I can't stop thinking about her. I'm thinking about her as I sit down to read my daughter to sleep! I'm thinking about who's with her over there—if it's Jeff Finney. I'm thinking I should have told her the story of Jeff's old man after all—just like this:

There had been a girl named Miranda Hessy. She was our age, and she looked normal but she was "a mute," and one rainy Friday she went missing. Her parents were out of their minds. Word dominoed through our school: The Mutant has been kidnapped! Some of us cut classes and went to help look for her. I ran to Jeff's house to tell him the news. He'd been home all week with the flu, but he grabbed his coat and we ran through the yards like the old days, like Jimbo was back. We were so sure we would find her!

We were wrong. Some adults found her at an empty house that was under repair. She was down in the furnace room with duct tape around her ankles and her wrists. She wasn't badly hurt but she had been messed with, we heard. "Things" had been put into her. Tools from the jobsite. The grip of a screwdriver. The haft end of a hammer. No tape, we heard, had been put over her mouth.

Two days later, Jeff Finney's dad was arrested, and my first thought was: Of course! Miranda Hessy wouldn't say "God Bless America!" and the old vet went nuts.

My father took on the case, doubling the weirdness for me at school: not just the friend of the son of the perv, now, but the son of the lawyer defending the perv. Some nights I heard my father talking to Jeff's mom on the phone, raising his voice so she'd hear him, and other times he'd horrify me by driving over to explain things in person: my dad, in Jeff Finney's house, in that kitchen, biting a school-made cookie. By this time Jeff had stopped coming to school, and I had stopped stopping by his house. Without a word, our friendship was done.

The trial lasted two weeks. The papers wrote about Vietnam and post-traumatic stress syndrome, and Jeff's old man was sent to crazy-prison, and Jeff never returned to school. Then, suddenly it was summer.

And what a summer! Six new vertical inches. Body hair. A compulsion to jump from diving boards at the first sign of cleavage. I don't believe I thought about Jeff's old man again until August, when my father told me he'd died in crazy-prison. The papers said "heart trouble," but we tanned and dripping teens knew he'd swallowed his tongue during shock treatment.

I went to the service with my father and got queasy when I saw Jeff Finney in his jacket and tie. He wouldn't look at me, not even when we went up to say how sorry we were. And the thing is, I was sorry. I had always secretly liked his old man, even after he put our dog to sleep.

I have read this story so many times to my daughter it's impossible to believe I was ever in love with it myself, that I could not hear it often enough in my father's voice, nor read it often enough when I learned to read. You could say I was obsessed with *Where the Wild Things Are*. Without knowing this about me, on our first Valentine's Day, Amy gave me a card with a Wild Thing cavorting on the cover. Inside was Max in his wolf suit: *"BE MINE, WILD THING!"* My heart had physically panged.

Now when I read the story to my daughter, my heart still pangs when we reach the words, "BE STILL!" but it is such a different pang.

I've just closed the book once again, and Lilly's lids are one droop away from lights-out—when the phone rings downstairs. She snaps awake and I hold my breath. We hear Amy mute the TV and pick up, mid-ring. There is no outcry of relief, nor any hint of the opposite. She says a few quiet words, listens, says a few more, and unmutes the TV.

False alarm, my darling. I kiss her forehead, her chin, her nose. She is the cleanest little thing on the planet.

"Daddy," she says before I can exit.

"Yes, sweetie."

"I'm scared."

"Why are you scared?"

"I'm scared Janie's scared. I'm scared she's alone and all hungry."

"Oh, but she's not, Lilly Goose."

"How do you know?"

The answer comes and I speak it without hesitation, with a confidence that is only possible, these days, in my daughter's room. "Because she's just off on a rumpus, sweetie. Like Max, you know—?" I stop short of mentioning Wild Things—so many monsters—but I should know better.

"I hope the Wild Things take good care of her," Lilly says, and I almost sob with love. "They will, Goose. They will."

She closes her eyes and I slip out and it's then, as I turn from my daughter's door, that I have my—event. I don't know what else to call it. It feels like a cold hand on the surface of my brain, twisting as if to open a lid. My eyes drop into darkness and my nostrils fill with scent—cut plywood, Cheetos—and when I can see again I'm in a small wooden room, staring at a woman.

What is that thing? I'm asking.

What thing? Jeff Finney is leaning forward.

That thing she's—she's—

Sticking in her cunt? I don't know, man. Just some thing to stick in her cunt. Give it here . . .

There's a second brain-twist, another dark passage, and I'm back—to myself, the top of my stairs, my hand on the banister.

I am thirty-seven and I have a family. A law practice. A well-built house . . . and Jeff Finney is in my life again. Is it supposed to go like this? Is it supposed to turn back on itself, to repeat? Have I done something to make this happen?

I descend the stairs carefully, trying to remember, to fathom. Was it a mistake, what happened to Jeff's old man—or worse, a lie? And was I part of it? I need to call my father, ask him some questions . . . but he's down in Florida now, and not doing great. His memory is going. And it's late.

"That was Carmen Wilson on the phone," says my wife. She doesn't take her eyes off the TV. A commercial. A wonder pill for men.

"Is she—" I say with a collapsed throat. "Did she—?"

"There's no news. She was just calling to let me know."

"Oh."

Amy turns to show me a mask of her face—pale and hard, her real eyes deep in the sockets. "Now why would she do that?"

I don't answer for a moment—a moment too long.

When she's ready, will you be?

"She needs to talk to someone, clearly," I say.

"Clearly."

"What does that mean?"

She turns back to the TV.

"You should go over there, Popeye. She needs you."

"Not funny," I say. "Under any circumstances."

She doesn't answer. The windows are wide open, I notice. Somebody's dog is barking hysterically, unceasingly—don't they hear it?

"I'm not going over there, Amy." I say. "Of course I'm not." This is what I say even as I begin to move toward the door. Is it the right thing to do? I don't know! I think of my son up in his room, drawing. How will he remember these days, the summer he was twelve? I imagine my own little girl's eyes—not Janie Wilson's, not Miranda Hessy's—filled with terror.

Jeff Finney is a house builder, I remind myself. He knows wood and structure and sound-proofing. He could've built an extra room into his house, a trap door, who would know? He could've built extra rooms into all our houses for all we know— spaces not on the blueprint, extra walls, oddities of layout we feel in our bones but never see.

Somebody needs to tell Carmen Wilson about this man, I tell myself. And who knows him better than me?

Lucky Gorseman

A river divides the campus now as ever, not equally, but so utterly that a citylike distinction can't be helped: East Side, West Side. The East Side is philosophy and English and art and music and no decent places to drink. This is my side. I live here in an 8-plex with a Russian poet I met the day I moved in and haven't seen since. He's got an American girlfriend on the West Side, the Russian poet does, so I don't take it personally. In fact everything good is over there: pizza, beer, dancing, undergrads, all the hard sciences. The West Side, some say, is the Best Side. But those who say it lack perspective, I think—or information. Certainly memory: few of them were here sixteen years ago; many were barely walking. Safe to say I'm the only one who was eleven and had a father who was on a hit-list but who, by the sheerest, dumbest luck imaginable, lived.

———————

Dad had been big in Canada for his work with comets, but what the Americans loved about him was his software. This was back in the day, when a computer was something. He taught himself code and wrote a program that, properly installed, would predict the trajectories of all the known large-body objects, or LBOs, of the solar system for the next 5,000 years, including (this was the juicy part) any potential Earth collisions. His impact scenarios were strictly "low probability-high consequence" affairs, and he did not dwell on consequences other than to size the hurtling objects relative to the (then-postulated) whopper that cooked the T-Rex crowd—but the program was still a hit. He named it "Trajectory Analysis and Prediction System" without a thought, he swore, to the acronym—and America came calling.

My mother and I climbed aboard and saw the States through the skewed lens of the visiting professor: Berkeley, Cambridge, Austin, Iowa City. We lived in the houses of other traveling egg-heads and slept in their beds. The public schools saved me a seat. Each town had its sky and each sky had its quirks and each quirk could only be properly studied (pondered, admired, loved) through the local megascope. While Dad did that, Mom and I walked. She'd been a topography student herself once upon a time, and her priority was always to know the land. She was a petite and mighty female strider and I was her huffing big fatty son. Likely she hoped to slim me down with so much walking, for my own sake, for the pounding I was taking in these American schools, but I came home to Hostess cakes and undid the mileage.

These were brainy, serious, proto-geek parents, and I was coming along nicely—until Iowa, my eleventh year, after which I began to drift away like space junk. I drifted so far that I came arcing back sixteen years later as a different kind of geek alto-gether: the writing kind.

Was it fate? Was it cosmic? No such thing in the movement of objects, Dad would say: only chances. There'd been a *small but nonzero chance* I would return to Iowa, he would say. And that had been enough.

───❧───

I admit I'm on tricky ground, here. Some days just the wind off the river, muscling over from the west, turns me into the anxious little porker I was. In writer's class I experience disabling fits of heartbeat whenever the girl across the way smiles. She's a smiler, is all, I tell myself; she's the grown-up model of a certain popular, empress type girl who would defend a tubby like me but never kiss him.

And yet, here she comes, one day, the smiler—right up to me after class to see if I want to join a small search party heading west.

"Across the river—?" I ask.

"For beers—?" she says.

And away we go. Walking again. She is the youthful spirit of my mother and she is taking me across the river and up the hill and on into a bar-and-grill I know too well, one block from Barnard Hall, the very bar-and-grill where my father would send me with quarters for the old arcade game (older than I was, this thing, with a sticky ball that left your hand smelling like ash, endless so-called asteroids coming at the little triangle that was you; so old, this thing, I expected it to do something spooky, like show me the future or make me old) while Dad finished up, up in the observatories, a gleaming roof-top pair my mother called the sky-knockers. Back into this time-capsule bar-and-grill we go, the smiler and I, to get a good beer buzz going and to fall the rest of the way in love before conversation turns unaccountably (though not, surely, unpredictably) to murder.

"... you know about that, right?" one of our party is saying. "That Chinese dude who shot those scientists? Walked into Barnard and shot like six dudes, then walked over to McClean and shot two women?"

"Not McClean," another says, "Lucas. My dad was in the math department, dude. He came home *white*."

The writers grow silent, the better to imagine the *clear, cyanic sky*, the *portly robins on the tender grass* while men bled from their heads in Barnard Hall. While the young man walked across the common, the gun in his jacket pocket like an apple, and shot a pretty girl in the mouth, then stepped into an empty classroom and fired lastly into his own brain. Their eyes light up with story, with prose potential, and I decide to hit the urinals (is it still back there, my old game, with the endless hurtling rocks; with my future self working the darkside of the sticky orb?) By the time I return they will have moved on from the topic of murder.

But.

I hesitate.

"And what about that one dude?" one of them says.

"What one dude—oh, the dude on the list?"

"Yeah, how lucky was that dude?"

"No kidding: goes to take a whiz, comes back to—that."

"Whiz? He wasn't taking a whiz."

"Sure he was," I say.

And this guy, this son of the math teacher, gives me a look.

"Dude had his fly open, friend, but not for pissing." He slides a glance over the smiling girl, my queen. "Dude was helping a grad student with her oral exams, if you'll pardon the expression."

The scene could not be more horrifying if I'd witnessed it myself with eleven-year-old eyes. Before me, the writers' faces grow huge, then small, then huge again. As if I'm sitting on a large ball rolling forward and back, forward and back.

"And you know this . . . *how?*" asks the girl. "Weren't you like, five?"

"I got this later, at a party. I heard my dad talking about it."

There is a smile in memory—only a smile, but vivid as any face: red lips parting on big white teeth up in the sky-knockers, a black little dot above the lip. It would follow me here, this smile, to the bar-and-grill, to bother me while I blasted space rocks.

Low probability, I think. *High consequence.*

"Who was she?" I demand on the forward roll.

"What?" He is disgusted by the question. "Just some grad student."

"Oh, man," says the young man to my right: "Dude was even luckier than I thought."

"Grossman!" blurts the son of the math teacher, and my head jerks as if struck. "'Lucky Grossman,' they called him."

"Hey," says the girl, touching my hand, "hey are you OK?" Her name is Sonny and there's a spray of tiny moles on her cheek bone in a pattern that would make anyone think of Orion. She touches my hand and something shifts, something sits up inside me like a devil. There's a hollowness to my hearing as I get to my feet.

"Not Grossman, friend," I tell the son of the math teacher. "Gorseman. First name, Richard."

The information bores in, one brain at a time: *Richard Gorseman* . . . until all their mouths are open like a choir. It's possible they find their voices while I'm still in earshot, they might be calling "Richard, hey Richard!" but it's too late, my tunnels are back. I thought I was done with them but here they are again: two long, coextending tubes full of hum and wind as I go crashing into daylight.

<hr />

The first time I got them—the tunnels—was in Principal Rath's office at Horace Mann Elementary, in Iowa. Principal Rath himself had come to fetch me and walk me mutely back to his office. A boy I recognized as the fellow son of a scientist was sitting in the outer room, and beside him sat the school nurse, her eyes fixed on his pale face. Principal Rath took me into his office and shut the door and told me there'd been an accident at the university, and that my mother was on her way. By the time I sat down next to the other boy I couldn't hear my fingers drumming my backpack. The nurse was asking me something but all I heard was a hum and a weird, celestial wind. I assumed the other boy had the same trouble.

Through these tubes I eventually understood my mother to say, "Dickey, say something, are you all right? Dickey, your father is fine. He wasn't one of those men."

And then, some days later: "Dickey, we need to talk. Your father . . . your father and I— Dickey, I'm going home for a while, back to Canada. I want you to come with me. If you want to."

One doctor poked around in my cochleas and sent me to another doctor who only wanted to chat, but who didn't seem to enjoy having to do it loudly. This chatting doctor concluded that what I needed most was a change of scenery, and he was right. The tunnels began to fall apart almost the instant we left town.

"Dickey sit up front, why don't you! It's hard to talk to you back there!"

"You don't have to yell, Dad." We were bridging high over another interstate, banking south.

"I don't? Well, that's great, buddy. But sit up here anyway, hey? It's hard to talk to you back there."

"So don't talk," I wanted to say. "Drive. Concentrate." I could hear again, but now the car was so altered, so out of whack with its two human passengers instead of three, it made me light-headed. I couldn't believe we wouldn't sail through the bridgeworks out into space. "It's a long drive, buddy," came his voice. "I wouldn't mind a little conversation."

No answer. I was watching the road. He had almost been killed in Iowa and didn't seem to notice; what else wouldn't he notice, if I wasn't there? I watched until I passed out, my head on the window, heading south, each mile another mile between us and Canada.

The next morning I woke up in a strange bed, in a strange room.

I walked down the hall and found him fully clothed, arms at his side, dead-center in a big white bed like a human bookmark. I waited, watching, until his chest rose, then I went downstairs to extract my bike from the minivan. He'd want a paper when he woke up. And a bag of doughnuts wouldn't kill either of us.

———◇———

We were in a subdivision, I saw when I got outside. House after identical house cooking under the Kansas sun. But I could hear again, and it was like having superpowers: I heard the sticky unzip of tire and asphalt; I heard chain links slipping over teeth like silky braces; I heard the very juice in the power lines. I rode to the end of the houses and braked into a skid. Before me across a blacktop road rose a wall of corn. I pulled out my Swiss compass and checked the needle. To the south, more subdivision. To the north, signs of humanity—possibly the campus. I turned for a last, memorizing look and saw that the subdivision had a name: *Forest View Village.* There was not a tree in sight.

I rode a long hot way before I realized the campus wasn't getting any closer. Blacktop heat seethed up into my sneakers, my fat neck was on fire. I was about to turn around when a noise reached my keen ears: the *bap-bap-bap* of a small engine, it sounded like, some distance behind me. Gaining ground.

I decided to keep going until whatever it was caught up and passed me. I decided to keep my eyes on the campus as the noise advanced—less like a motor now than a stick being dragged along a picket fence. I watched the campus as a shadow appeared to my right on the blacktop, and a second one flanked me to the left, and I knew it didn't matter what I did, I was fucked. I readied for a stick in the spokes, a shower of loogies, but in the next instant a car slashed by with a scream of horn that made me weave. "Watch it, kid!" the rider on my right barked, while the other lurched ahead on my left, flinging his middle finger after the car. "Suck on this, bitch!" he wailed, "ass-fucker!" He was not a big kid, I noted. Skinny as the center line.

The other kid, the one making the *bap-bap-bap* noise, pulled even to give me a look at his Asian eyes and his strange, Popsicle-red mouth. He was bigger than the other one (though still not as big as me; few were) and the sleeves had been ripped from his T-shirt to expose the full brown twitch of his arms. Both kids wore long jeans, in contrast to my khaki shorts with the deep pockets full of pens and notebooks and the Swiss compass.

"Can you believe that?" the Asian-eyed kid said. A playing card was clamped to the fork of his bike by some kind of pliers. Spokes moved the card like a flip-the-pages book with the same drawing on every page. It was a face card.

Be cool, I told myself.

"Believe what?"

"Her *mouth*, man. She's got her dad's ass and her mom's mouth, too bad for her."

"I heard that, Miago." The forward kid craned around and re-aimed the bird and my heart crashed against blacktop: a girl. A starved-skinny girl with boy hair, shoving her finger at me and Miago.

"Don't call me that, Mule," said the boy. "I warned you."

"Don't call me Mule." She allowed us to catch up with her, then rode close to my left. "He's sensitive 'cause he's half-chink," she told me. Her mouth was full of crooked teeth.

"God damn it, Mule."

"And adopted."

The boy's face took on the Popsicle hue of his lips, and his whole body seemed to tremble, and I understood, I understood exactly—

"What're you staring at, you fat fuck?" he said, and I looked away, burning.

"What's your name?" the girl asked.

I didn't hesitate. "Richard."

"So what do they call you—Richie? They call you Richie Rich, like the comic?"

"Maybe they call him Dick," the boy speculated.

Close, I thought.

"Naw," said the girl. "I think it's Richie. Look at this Schwinn. Looks brand new, Richie."

"I just cleaned it," I said. In fact it was new: a gift from my mother before she left for Canada. A bike and a compass—in case I changed my mind?

"Really? Damn." The girl regarded her own rusted, rattling Huffy. "I oughta clean mine, huh?"

"'Cept it ain't yours," the boy said.

"'*Cept it ain't yours*," she said, making a face: buck-toothed, squinty-eyed.

"Watch it, Mule," he said.

Ahead, beyond the corn, were oak trees and a traffic light and a university-looking building blazing white in the sun. I could count the number of telephone poles between here and there; I could count the seconds it took to get from one pole to the next— yet I didn't seem to be getting any nearer at all. As if the trees, the traffic light, the white building, all moved as I moved, forever the same distance away, like the horizon itself. Like the sun.

The girl began to whistle, a listless *Hi-ho, hi-ho, it's off to work we go*. She whistled until blackbirds startled from the corn, then smacked herself hard on the forehead. "I got it!"

"What?" said the boy.

She swerved and hit her brakes, forcing me to do the same or collide. The boy stopped too and in the abrupt silence I heard a note in my head, the distant high tone of a hearing test. Were the tunnels coming back?

No: the girl gripped my handle bar and I clearly heard: "My name's Jewel, Richard, and this is James and we're not gonna fuck with you, we just want to show you something. OK?" There were black spots in her blue eyes, I saw. Like little dark moons.

"Not prudent," said James. "What if he narcs?"

"What's to narc?" she said, and he stared at her for a long moment, until she rolled her eyes and said: "OK, Richard, for *his* sake, you gotta promise to keep this secret."

What else can you do? You promise.

"Swear to God and hope to die?"

I nodded.

"Say it."

I dipped my head, said the words—and on we rode, doggedly, toward the horizon.

There were nine poles to go to the trees, the traffic light, the white building—270 seconds!—when the girl, Jewel, banked suddenly as if to run me off the blacktop, and I turned and went jouncing onto a surprise dirt road—two dirt tracks like train rails into the corn, into a vegetable tunnel. The noise from the playing card became deafening. Nobody talked. Grasshoppers jumped into our path and leapt away again, their little hearts exploding. Then, at some landmark I never saw, James braked and dumped his bike. Jewel did the same, then stood by the corn as if holding open a door. "This way, Richard."

It was dusk in there. No shadows to tell you where the sun was, and after a few turns among the rows I lost my bearings. I touched my pocket for the shape of the Swiss compass. *Be cool*, I thought. *You are not afraid*, I thought.

Then I caught the smell: gaseous, rich, livestock stink—with something else mixed in, putrid, like the house in Austin after we set out the poison, dead rats in the walls. James spun to face me and I jumped, and he laughed. He said something I didn't hear and walked on. He made a few more turns and stepped suddenly into sunlight. Blinded, I almost stepped over the edge, into space—a ravine, a long gash in the landscape. On the far side was a mud pasture strewn with caked, wallowing pigs.

"Is it still there?" Jewel asked, joining us.

"Can't you smell?" James said.

"Come on, Richard. Down here." She grabbed my wrist and pulled me down. The crease of the ravine was also a fence line, I saw, long neglected. At one point the barbed wire had sagged under a mound of earth. But then Jewel began swatting the air and I realized it wasn't a mound of earth at all, it was a pig. An enormous black sow, her back a field of brilliant green points, all in motion. Buzzing filled my ears like sand.

"God, look at those flies," Jewel said. "I thought they only liked cow shit."

She had let go but the feel of her fingers still handcuffed my wrist.

"They're laying eggs," I said.

"How do you know?"

I adjusted my glasses. "See how swelled the body is? When the insides decompose, the body fills with hot gas. The heat is good for the eggs."

"No kidding?" she said, and I liked the way she said it. I moved closer and squatted. I studied the body without looking at the face.

"She got caught in the wire," I reported. "And the more she struggled the more it cut her."

"That right?" Jewel's tone had changed, and when I looked she was glancing up, to where James had been, and now wasn't. She turned back, scratching her jaw like a man, like my father when he didn't shave.

You should get back, buddy, I thought. *You should be there when he wakes up.*

"I thought a pig was supposed to be so smart," she said. "A pig's supposed to be smarter than a dog but you know what? I never seen a dog yet get his head caught in bob-wire."

I turned back to the pig. But there was the wire, sunk into the fat of the neck, and the wounds . . .

It was one wound, in fact. A single deep slit, the edges curled back like lips. The cut of a blade.

I stood and took a step away. "The farmer did that," I said, but the words dropped into a well. I looked up and the ravine was higher and steeper. The sky was a far-off rung of blue.

"The farmer, huh?" said Jewel.

I took another step away. "She'd've died anyway." I sunk my hands in my pockets and felt the contents. I found a Bic pen and held it. "She was suffering."

Jewel watched me. She scratched at the snarl of her hair. "Kid," she said. "Where you from?"

"Canada," I said.

"Canada?" I might've said the moon, or Andromeda. "What're you doing here?" she said, and I stared at the sky and explained my father's job, the way we moved from town to town. I didn't mention the fact that he was a famous scientist or that my mother had gone back to Canada, and Jewel wasn't listening anyway, she was staring at the pig, a dent of concentration between her eyes.

"What's the most fucked-up thing you ever saw?" she abruptly asked, and I didn't know what to say—could I say *This, right here—?*

"One time," she said, "I saw this old boy fall out of a truck on the highway. Cracked his head like a pumpkin. Another time I seen a cat lit on fire and screaming like a lady." She watched me for a reaction. Was I having one? "Most fucked-up thing ever, though? I saw a man hit a lady with his belt thirty times. He counted 'em out loud."

At some point I'd begun to stare at her T-shirt—at the two formations in the field of dingy white. The new small hills of her body. I stared even after I knew that she knew I was staring, and I knew I should look away, and yet I didn't, and she just stood there, stroking her forearm lightly, until at last I glanced down and saw the scar, pearly and crescent-shaped, a smile of the arm.

"One time?" I said, "when we lived in Iowa? This Chinese guy, this graduate student, walked into a conference room and started shooting people. He shot four people and kept shooting till they were all dead. Then he walked across campus and shot these two ladies. Then he shot himself in the head."

Jewel fixed her eyes on me, with a warning: she was not the person you wanted to fuck with.

"Why'd he do it?" she said.

"He didn't win this grant thing," I said. "He wrote a letter to his sister, about how everybody was against him. He had a list of people to kill." I thought of the folds of newspaper I could show her. The secret bookmarks stashed in my books.

Jewel attacked a fingernail with her crooked teeth. "But you didn't see that. You didn't see them bodies."

I shook my head. "But my dad did. My dad went to the bathroom down the hall just before the grad student came in," I said. "He was on the list, my dad," I said.

"God Damn," said Jewel. "How lucky is that?"

My eyes filled with stinging heat. "Lucky—?"

"Shit yes. He waits one second to piss and it's lights out, Jack." She stared off dreamily, and I had the bewildering impulse to pick her up—to literally *pick her up* and carry her back to the road like a hurt dog, back to houses and people.

Instead here was the Swiss compass in my fist, warm and heavy. I was pulling it out, ready to give it to her, when something struck me in the neck. A small rock out of the sky. A skimpy asteroid.

"What're you doing, Mule?"

We both looked up. He was back.

"Talking," she said. "What's it to you?"

"What about?"

"None a your business."

"Hell it's not." He casually flung another small rock at me. "What're we gonna do with fatty?"

"I don't know." Jewel turned back to me. "What're we gonna do with you, Richard?"

"I don't know," I answered. "It's not predictable," I could've added.

"You are fat," she said. "But could be you're good luck." She came forward and I flinched. "It's all right," she said. Her hand was out. I stared at it, at the pink moon on her forearm. I let go of the compass and took her hand. It was bony and hot and the moment I touched it I wanted to cry—not out of fear or relief or anything I could name. It was just a feeling, a white pulse that traveled from her fingers up my arm and into my chest like a point of light. Like the visible light from a star already dead.

⚬⚬⚬

Once, during the worst of my days, when I would bar the door with the dead weight of myself each time he attempted to go back to work, back to the sky-knockers, my father sent the following down my ear tunnels: "Imagine, son: this planet, as it spins around the sun? It passes through the orbits of thousands of asteroids and comets, and the last one that even came close to hitting us missed by four million miles!"

"What about the ones we can't even see?" I yelled back. "You said millions!"

He smiled down at me. "I know I did. But I'm talking about odds, Dickey. Imagine that sick boy as a comet. No, just imagine it, please. He happened, by chance, to collide with Earth. There was an impact. A horrible one. Now imagine a second comet not only with the exact same trajectory, but so close behind that it will strike again in our lifetime. Do you see what I'm saying?"

I nodded. "Except."

"Except what?"

"Except he wasn't a comet, Dad. He was a grad student."

———

I waited a long time with that dead pig. Was it a trick? Would they get me in the corn? I waited until I could hear nothing but the flies in my ears, then I said "I'm sorry" to the pig and scrambled up the incline. I made my way without compass or sun, and I wasn't surprised when I emerged on the dirt road just a few yards from where I'd left my bike. I wasn't surprised, either, that it was gone. A playing card lay on the spokes of the Huffy, set there carefully. The Jack of spades, the one-eyed Jack, bearing the teeth-marks of those pliers. I slipped it in my pocket with my other stuff, then picked up the Huffy and began to ride. It was a pretty good bike, actually, and in no time I was back on the blacktop and heading home. I sailed into Forest View Village and dumped the Huffy in the yard and flung myself into the house calling *"Dad! Dad!"*

"Right here!"

He was in the kitchen, at the table. He'd shaved his face and combed his hair. He'd found the coffee and made himself a pot.

"What is it, Dickey? Is it your ears—?"

"No. I just—" I caught my breath. I tried to calm my fat heart. *Here he was. Everything was fine.*

"You just what?"

I walked over and sat down.

"I don't want you to call me that anymore," I said. "OK?"

———

There wasn't much thrust left after Kansas. Not even the notoriety of freakish good luck could compete with the flashier prediction systems coming out, and my father landed finally in the Nevada desert, accepting a fixed position among fixed men, and I braced for another year of school. Six months later I was summoned to the principal's office and given the news I'd been waiting for since Iowa: my father had dodged a bullet but it didn't matter. His heart had come apart anyway—suddenly, quietly, at his computer in the desert.

I was put on a plane with his body and returned to Winnipeg for the burial, where I cried but would not permit my mother to touch me. Later, as we were getting used to each other again, she told me he'd tried hard to get her back, and she wondered if she'd been too hard, too cold. I patted her shoulder as she wept, and it was the best I could do. I didn't know which upset me more—that he'd tried and failed to get her back, or that I never knew about it, or that she'd told me. I didn't know then about graduate students and professors. I didn't know everything going on in the name of science, and she would not be the one to tell me. To predict where objects in space are going you need to know where they've been. All I knew at twelve was that a young man could show up one day and start shooting people in the head, and that that was reason enough to go back to Canada, to leave your husband and son to fight for themselves.

Up There

"Wake up, princess," she whispered, and her face surfaced white, spectral, from out of the dark, eyes dark and glittering.

He looked away, beyond her, into the strangeness of the room: the outline of a little desk, the black gleam of a TV. His blood was pumping hard from a dream. When he spoke, his troubled face seemed to be saying, *Where am I? What is this place?* but what he said was: "Timezit?"

The air was very dry. His tongue was a lizard in the dry socket of his mouth. Above him, the smile broke slowly, sweetly, in the white face as it retreated, as it withdrew into darkness again and the darkness healed over it like water.

"Time to run," said her voice.

———

Outside, the sun was still climbing the far side of the mountains, and the valley waited in cold blue shadow. Clouds shredding pink in the toothy peaks, the moon still luminous in the west. No one was around, no one to see the two of them passing under a blinking yellow traffic light going *d-dink, d-dink, d-dink* just for them. They drew the air in and coughed up white clouds. The smell of pine was like Christmas. The girl was not yet running but high-stepping in a soundless pantomime of it, like a horse, or a drum majorette for a parade that consisted of the boy alone,

slow and awobble behind her on the rented bike. The boy wanted
to go back for sweatshirts but the girl shook her ponytail: it would
warm up. It was August, she reminded him.

Their names were Caitlin and Shawn Courtland, but they
called each other Dudley—a one-time insult that had lost its
meaning. They'd come into the small resort town the day before,
up from the plains, up over the divide and down again—*down*
to nine-thousand feet. Lift chairs hanging empty over the grassy
runs. Air like they had never breathed before. It was all the
girl's idea, her choice, a graduation gift from their parents. In
a few weeks she would begin college, on track scholarship, and
although she'd never said it aloud she was sure that the girls at
college would be faster and stronger, more experienced and more
determined, than her. When she saw the mountains for the first
time from the car, when her brain undid the illusion of some dark
and massive sea wave on the horizon, her heart began to pump
and the muscles in her legs had flexed and twitched.

Now she turned north up a blacktop called Ermine and began
to run in earnest, and the boy bore down on his pedals.

The road climbed gradually at first, then with increasing turns
and steepness through the tall pines. Above it ran a purple cursive
of sky, pinholed by dimming stars. The girl ran effortlessly, deer-
like, her bare legs livid with the blood in them, and the boy began
to fall behind—the bike lurching and ratcheting in mechanical
palsy as he clicked through the gears. In no time he was sweating.
He couldn't get this air into his lungs. "Slow down!" he cried. He
watched his own quivering thighs for five, six turns, and when he
looked up again she had stopped.

He came laboring up and planted his feet. "Dudley—"
he gasped.

"Shh," she said. Her chest was heaving too but she was
smiling, outbreaks of bright red on her cheeks. Her burning
lungs, her galloping heart were ecstasies to her. At home, across

a wall of her room, track ribbons lay feathered like the wing of a brilliant bird. "Do you see it?" she said.

"What?"

"Up there."

"What?"

"Just off the road. He's right there."

Then he saw it: a small red dog with a thick tail stuck straight out behind. But not a dog. Something wild, something wary, with black little eyes and great cocked ears.

"What is it?" he said.

"I think it's a fox."

"No, it's too big. Isn't it? What's in his mouth?"

"I don't know."

"It's a baby," he said. "It must be her baby."

"No, it's dead. There's blood."

"Maybe she killed her baby."

They stared at the fox and the fox stared back, until something stirred in the trees and the fox about-faced, that limp small freight swinging in its jaws, and went loping up the road. After a time, at some unknown sign, it veered into the woods and vanished.

"Wow," they both said.

The girl wanted her water and the boy shucked off the backpack and extracted the two spouted bottles. She'd stopped not because of the fox but because she'd come to an intersection and was unsure of the way. The guy at the bike shop (with the tattoo spider climbing his neck, the eyebrow stud, the green eyes) said there'd be signs, but there weren't, not here.

They shot cold water into their mouths and the boy removed his helmet and they unfolded the map between them.

"That way," she said, indicating the gravel road leading up the mountain.

"That's not right. We said we were going to stay on county roads. Mom said we had to."

"Dudley," said the girl. She jammed her bottle back into the pack. "Did you rent a *mountain* bike so you could ride around on county roads?"

——

It was seven o'clock in the morning, one half-hour since the boy and the girl left the hotel, and now their father awoke into the strange darkened room: the little desk, the dark TV. His groin was aching. He'd drunk too much soda the night before at dinner, then fallen asleep watching some horror show with the boy and slept through the night, a rare thing for him.

He was a long time at the toilet and a short while at the sink, brushing his teeth, noting the little moat of water around the boy's brush, the blue scab of paste around the trunks of the bristles. He splashed his face and returned to the room, to the window. The sky was a perfect early dark blue, only a few thin clouds grazing the distant peaks. Some far-off bird, hawk or kite, rode the thermals, hanging there for the longest time before at last falling as if shot, dropping missile-shaped into the trees and disappearing. He watched but it did not return to the sky.

He wasn't sure where the kids were, geographically. It might be that mountain there, those trees, which looked so close. They had all bent over the map the night before, but he had not looked closely; it was their adventure to plan and to carry out.

He stared into the distance until he thought he saw something—a wink of chrome, a flash of white running shoes. But there was nothing, of course, only the green repeating pattern of trees.

He picked up his cell phone and entered a number, a full number—but then hesitated, his thumb hovering, riding the thermals over the send button. The taste of skin came to him, the very taste of a pale long throat bared to his mouth. He folded the phone shut and set it down again, and stared at it, as though it might now ring in reply. He flattened a hand to his chest and held it there, waiting.

———— ❧ ————

The path grew narrower, less a gravel road now than a pair of ruts twisting up the mountain, and soon these became a single snaking ravine, all the gravel and sand washed away leaving behind only this bald jawbone of stones—a stream, it was, the dry bed of a mountain stream meant to carry melting snows down and nothing up. "This isn't right!" the boy called ahead, but the girl kept going, dodging between the stones. He struggled on, wheezing, his jaw jangling on its hinge and all his upper body jello-ing horribly, until at last he said "Fuck this" and let the bike bump to a stop, then let it fall clattering to the stones as he staggered away.

"Caitlin!" he yelled. Panting, sweating. His legs took an unexpected step. He felt enormous and weightless. Some whirring thing struck his helmet, shrilled a moment in the vents and sped away. "God damn you," he said.

He picked up the bike and began pushing it up the stream bed. But in another moment he was attacked again—something under the pack now, buzzing huge against his back, and in a frenzy he dropped the bike and began to twist from the straps before he understood it was her phone, Caitlin's phone, and by the time he had the pack off and the phone in his hand the buzzing had stopped. He watched the little window for the new message alert— but it never came. He checked his own phone, then dropped both phones back into the pack. Then he picked hers out again. Bright, lacquer-red in his hand, red like nail polish, like lipstick.

He sat on a stone with his back to the mountain and punched up a series of text messages and read them there in the deep seam of the pines, his heart thumping. But the most interesting thing about them were the names: *Colby. Allison. Natalie. Amber.* Lean, well-breasted girls who arrived in track shorts to drink his Diet

Cokes and laugh, and talk, and talk, and talk. The time he sat out-side the basement window and heard Allison Chow tell the other girls about her boyfriend's big thing almost choking her. The time he walked in on Colby Wilson in the bathroom, bare-thighed on the toilet. Track shorts and panties pushed to the knees.

Nice knock, tubs.

—

There was a wash of sunlight up ahead, the trees dropping away as if bulldozed. It was a road, a blacktop as smooth and clean as the one they'd first been on at the bottom of the mountain. He found a sign on the road that said *CO Rd. 153* and he found the sun on his hot neck and he found little purple flowers growing along one edge of the blacktop. But no Caitlin.

He looked up the road to where it swung out of sight again, and down the other way to where it fell away like a plummeting ride. He called her name one way and then the other. He decided to go up, because she would be moving slower, and if he didn't see her around the bend he would ride back down to that crest, and if he didn't see her from there he would get out his phone and call their father.

He had not gone far when something burst from the trees, some roaring upright thing that made him leap from the bike heart exploding and run. It only lasted a moment before he heard her donkey-laugh, and the blood came boiling to his face.

"God damn you," he said.

"Oh god, Dudley, you should've seen your face!"

He picked up the bike. He didn't look at her. His heart was raging.

"I never knew you could move so fast!" she said.

"I never knew you could be such a cunt," he said.

She stopped laughing—and a man's voice filled in from some-where. From everywhere. In a moment it broke decidedly over the rise below them, and behind it came two figures, helmeted and hunched over their bikes, a man and a woman. The man stopped talking when he saw them there and he and the woman came on in winded silence, legs pistoning, red-faced. The man said Howdy to the boy and the boy said Howdy back. One of the man's lower legs was not a real leg but a black post locked into a special pedal, so that it was hard to say where the bike ended and the man began. When they had rounded the bend and were gone again, the girl said, "What did you call me?"

Her face was burning. So was his.

"Christ, Caitlin. I was *looking* for you. We were *supposed* to keep an eye on each other."

She stared at him coal-eyed, jaw muscles pulsing. But in a moment she shook her head. She adjusted the band at the root of her ponytail and came forward and he flinched—and she told him she did have her eye on him, she knew exactly where he was the whole time, what kind of person did he think she was?

He stood studying the oily, pebbled texture of the road, his heart thudding.

She watched him, giving him a moment.

"Do you want to see something?" she said.

"What."

"You'll see." And she walked back into the pines.

—✦—

He pulled on a pair of jeans, a T-shirt, and walked barefoot into the adjoining room. Both beds empty and tossed like the sites of struggles. The room, which had been so cold when the girls went to bed, was now hot and reeking faintly of stale perfume and sweat. They had woken in the night burning, throwing off layers. He went to see that the heating unit was off, then crossed to the small staging area outside the bathroom where the two suitcases lay on racks, gaped like autopsies, their insides distinguished at a glance by the colors and cuts of underthings, bras and panties.

A vertical seam of light ran along the bathroom door, emitting steam and the steady rasp of a toothbrush. He widened it and there she stood at the mirror, barefoot in the steam, wearing a large red T-shirt that shimmied skirt-like at her bare thighs. It was one of those glimpses that pulled up into the chest the feeling of what it had once been like, years ago, when everything about her was new, even her name—Angela Newberry. College days. Her little apartment on Fairchild over the bakery ovens. Winter mornings in bed with the smell of her, the smell of baking bread, almost more than his heart could take. She'd had a twin sister named Faith who drowned when they were sixteen, and he could not imagine such a thing. He was reading books then, literature, with no clear explanation or plan. Then came pregnancy, bills, real life. He went to work for a builder and she stayed in school, sometimes taking the baby with her to class when Mrs. Turgeon was sick. The baby eighteen, now. A young woman. Going to college. Blink of an eye.

She saw him there, staring through the steam.

"Fan dudn't wuk," she said around the toothbrush, and he came to stand behind her. His face looming in the portal she'd wiped in the glass, totemed on top of hers. Dark jaw and dark thinning hair, eyes socketed deep by the overhead light.

"You dressed," she said.

Her hair was wet and drawn by her comb into many neat, agrarian rows from which rose a clean smell of fruit. They watched each other. The sound of the brushing grew acute, nuanced, the bristles relaying like sonar the shape and placement of each tooth.

"Did they call you yet?" he asked, and she bent to spit, bumping her backside into him. She rinsed and brushed, bent over. "Not yet," she said. Spit. "But it's early." She stood again and found his eyes in the glass. "Another hour, I'd say. Easy."

"You missed some." He touched the corner of his lip and she put a matching finger to her own lip, dragging it down a little, disclosing a white lower canine. "You need to rinse better," he said.

"It's a fault of mine." She bent again to the sink, the running water. Bumping him again. He gathered the strands of damp hair into a single rope and held it for her while she rinsed. The v-neck of the red T-shirt gaped in the mirror, opening a view down the pale front of her. She turned off the water and flattened her hands to either side of the sink. He lifted and collected the T-shirt into the scoop of her back and gazed down on her, on the round, smooth, proffered white buttocks.

"Grant," she said.

His hands here, upon her, holding her, were like things forged in some furnace, pulled huge and dark and ruined to rest here, to cool and heal on these pale surfaces.

"Yes," he said.

"Let's go lie down. I want to see your face."

⸺⸺

She walked back into the pines and the boy followed, and soon they were surrounded by the tall bonewhite bodies of aspens, a subforest within the forest. There was a footpath, and at the end of the footpath was a clearing, a sylvan grotto within which there stood, waiting for them, the Virgin Mary. Life-sized, marble smooth, purely white. Around her had been built a crude housing, a carapace of stones and mortar. Two fingers of her right hand, raised in a saint's greeting, were severed at the second knuckle, giving her less an air of beneficence than of astonishment, as if she'd been sculpted in that instant before blood and panic.

"Did you see that?" the boy said, pointing to the hand.

"I know, right? Like Dad's."

"What's it doing up here, do you think?"

"I'm guessing it has something to do with those," and she pointed to where a cluster of small chalky headstones rose from the forest floor, each at its own tilt as if growing toward a particular cant of sunlight. Corralling them was a failing squat fence of iron and rust.

There was a stone bench next to the Virgin, and they sat down to drink water and eat waxy energy bars in the mottled shade.

"Who do you think they were?" the boy asked, and the girl shrugged and said, "Settlers."

"Donner party," said the boy.

"That's California. Look, there's a plaque." She bent a sprig of juniper at the base of the stone shelter to expose a bronze plate and its verdigrised inscription:

> *Right Reverend Tobias J. Fife,*
> *Bishop of Denver, Mercifully Grants*
> *In The Lord, An Indulgence Of*
> *Forty Days For Visiting The Shrine*
> *And Praying Before It,*
> *1937.*

"The right reverend," said the girl. "I like that."

"What's an indulgence of forty days?"

"I think it means you don't have to pray again for forty days. Like a vacation."

"Maybe it means you're safe for forty days. Nothing bad can happen to you."

"Maybe. Hand me my phone."

The boy reached into the pack and handed her the red phone. She checked for messages, then flipped it open, aimed, and took a picture of the shrine.

They sat listening to the leaves. A cooling breeze came to touch the backs of their necks. The boy chewed on the energy bar and made a gagging sound, and the girl told him not to eat it on her account, and raised an eyebrow at him.

"Go ahead," she said. "I won't tell."

He tossed the energy bar into the pack and fished into the cargo pocket of his shorts and fetched up the big Snickers and began to peel back the wrapper. "Want some?" he said.

"Absolutely." She took the bar and opened her mouth as if to jam the whole thing in, but then only clipped a little off with her front teeth. He ate the remainder in three great bites, mouth open, chewing and gasping. He took a long drink of water and caught his breath. He drummed his fingers on the backpack and stared at the Virgin's truncated fingers. Their mother believed in God but their father said they had to make up their own minds.

"Can I ask you something?" he said.

"It's a free country," she said.

"Do you think Dad's screwing around?"

She leaned away from him slowly, and twisted at the waist, and beheld him from this new vantage.

"*What?*" she said.

"Don't you think he's been acting kind of weird lately?"

"Yeah, for like the last twenty years. How do you go from that to *screwing around?*"

The boy shrugged. He gazed obscurely into the aspens. "I saw something. A while ago."

She narrowed her eyes at him. "Saw what?"

It was at their father's office, the steel building out of which he ran his contractor's business. The boy had been there doing his chores: cleaning, sweeping, putting away tools. But one of the chests was locked and he'd gone back to get the key, and the office door was open. And.

The girl stared at him. "And what?"

The boy dug audibly at the back of his neck. His face was red again. "And he was sitting there. And there was a girl. In there."

"A girl?"

"A woman. Sitting on his desk. Like on his side of the desk? And she was wearing a skirt."

The girl waited a moment. "And what else?"

"Nothing else."

"That's all she was wearing?"

"No! That's all I saw."

"Jesus Christ, Shawn." She stood up. She brushed at the stone bench as if it were covered with insects. Sat down again. "Then what happened?"

"Nothing. He saw me, and the woman got off the desk, and he said she was a client. She shook my hand and went away."

"So what gave you this *screwing around* idea?"

"I don't know! Shit." He wrung the pack in his hands like it was someone's forearm. "Just forget it. Let's get outta here."

She stood again and looked down on him. His worried, pink soft face. She swept at her bottom and walked toward the graves. The boy glanced at the Virgin and got up quickly and followed.

She stood at the edge of the little graveyard with her arms crossed, an elbow in each palm. The heat was leaving her body. She needed to get running again. The boy was standing beside her.

"I shouldn't have said anything," he said.

She was silent, rubbing her arms. She thought vaguely of a poem she had read the night before. And then she told him about the time their father had stopped living with them—three, maybe four months in all, though it had seemed much longer. The boy had been small, just learning to walk. Their mother told her it was nothing to worry about, but Caitlin had heard the way she spoke to him on the phone, she remembered her face. She remembered the words, too, but she didn't repeat them now.

She fell silent and the boy stared at the old tombstones, blurring in his hot eyesight. The white aspens like great bones rising from the soil.

"When he finally came back home," the girl went on, "his fingers were missing. I always thought that was why he came back—because wherever he'd been was a place where you lost your fingers."

"He used to tell me—" the boy swallowed. "He used to say they fell off from smoking."

"And you believed him."

He didn't answer. In an instant everything was different—each one of them.

"What do you think will happen this time?" he asked, and the girl released a breath that seemed to stir the little spangle leaves of the aspens like toneless chimes, a sound like rain.

"Nothing," she said. "Don't worry," she said.

—✸✸✸—

The curtains over the window were drawn and all the lamps were off but the room was not dark. Daylight leached from the curtains in yellow wings along the wall and upward, a bright crown throwing a range of ceiling texture into stark relief like some minute Arctic range. Grant, naked under the bedsheet, stared at this, thinking. He'd dozed a few minutes, but then popped awake with his chest tight, his heart pumping. For a moment he hadn't known what bed he was in. Whose arm lay across his stomach.

You have made a grave mistake, he lay there thinking. But the words were like something he'd read in a book, that word *grave*.

In the next moment there was a gasp, a spasm, and his wife said, "No—" and he said, "It's all right," and touched her shoulder. She still dreamt, sometimes, of her twin.

"—What?" She lifted her head, her brown eyes.

"You said 'no.'"

She drew the hair from her face, unsticking it from her lips. "I did?"

"Yes."

She shifted, and resettled her head on his chest. She breathed.

"Your heart is beating," she said.

"That's a relief."

Somewhere a door slammed and a joyful stampede shuddered the hallway, many small bare feet racing for the pool, the high summer voices.

"It's going to be weird. Isn't it," she said. She was looking beyond him to the other bed. The twisted heap of bedding, the illusory suggestion of a body within it. She spread her hand on his chest.

"What is?"

"You know what."

He regarded the empty bed. "It went fast," he said.

"That's what everyone tells you: You won't believe how fast it goes. In a few years, Shawnie too." She sighed.

She tapped a finger twice on his chest, like a soft knock. She did it again.

"Don't even think it, Angela."

"We're not too old. I'm not."

"I am," he said, and she said, "No, it keeps you young."

In the room next door a woman began a violent hacking. A TV came to life, an anchorman's voice, some urgent new development in the world.

"They saved some money on these walls," Grant said.

"Was I loud? Earlier?"

"I don't give a damn," he said.

"Me either."

They left the aspens and stepped back into a pure high sunlight, their shadows thrown back upon the blacktop. The last of the morning had burned off. The air was sere and smelled of oozing sap and brown, desiccated needles. Everything on the brink of combustion. They unfolded the map and spent some time getting their bearings. In a moment, and for the first time that day, they heard an engine, and then a gaining thumpbeat of music, and a moment later above them at the bend, with a burst of volume, there banked into view a car, or a truck, or something in-between, some mountain breed they didn't know, and it was coming and Caitlin said "Get over here" and the boy crabwalked himself and the bike into the scrub and wildflowers while the strange vehicle, all sunlight and bass, veered wide of them. In the window a face, a man's jaw, dark eyes fixed on them for a long moment before the vehicle passed on and, reaching the crest of the road, vanished as if over a cliff.

They set off again, uphill, and when they came around the bend there was another road, unpaved, intersecting the blacktop at an oblique angle, like an X, and Caitlin simply took it. And although the road was unmarked, and although it appeared as though it would take them higher up rather than down, the boy said nothing. Later, he would think about that, his silence. He would remember the shrine in the aspens. The graves. He would see the Virgin's face, her mutilated blessing, and he would remember thinking that they should pray before her anyway, like the plaque said, just in case. But Caitlin had already been on the path, moving toward the road. She was wearing a white sleeveless top, white shorts with the word BADGERS across her bottom, and white sneakers, and for a moment, in that place, she had looked not like herself but some blanched, passing ghost. A cold wanderer around whom the air chilled, and the birds shuddered, and the leaves of the aspens yellowed and fell.

———

He swung out his legs and sat with a scrap of bedsheet over his lap. His right leg bouncing, dandling an invisible child, trembling the floor.

"There's nothing to do, Grant," she said to his bare back, the pale map of muscle and bone. Moles like a dark constellation. There was something about being in a strange place that made everything more vivid, more exceptional. "You are far away in a magical land where nobody works," she said.

He lifted the water bottle from the night stand and drank. "They'll be back soon, though."

"Yes. And we wouldn't want them to catch us in bed. Would we."

His heart took a skip. "No." He set the bottle on the nightstand—and saw the book there. Small, hardbound, face-down on its pages. He lifted it, trapping his thumb in the crease, and inspected the cover.

"Are you reading this?"

"It's Caitlin's."

"Where'd she get it?"

"Someone gave it to her."

"Who?"

"I don't know."

"It's D. H. Lawrence. Did you know that?"

"Yes. So?"

"So I didn't know she read this kind of stuff." He spread the book and read the block of typescript to the left of his thumb:

> *WHEN the wind blows her veil*
> *And uncovers her laughter*
> *I cease, I turn pale.*
> *When the wind blows her veil*
> *From the woes I bewail*
> *Of love and hereafter:*
> *When the wind blows her veil*
> *I cease, I turn pale.*

"What kind of stuff?" Angela asked.

Grant returned the book carefully, face-down, to the night-stand. "Poetry," he said.

He turned to look at her. "Is something funny about that?"

She shrugged. She shook her head. "Shall we call them?"

"In a minute."

"We'd better call them," she said.

"I'm going to open up these curtains."

"I know. I'm ready."

⸎

She lay there a while longer getting used to the light, watching the shape of him, like a cut-out before the window. His exact familiar outline. He stood a naked dark sculpture of himself before the sun and the world and at last she went to him, and put her arms around his hips, and pressed herself to him. To skin that no longer smelled of smoke, or alcohol, but only of him. "Someone will see," she said, but beyond them, out the window, there was nothing but the sky and the mountains, peaked and stacked to the horizon in diminishing brilliances of green.

He had her phone in hand, beeping through the menu. She told him "Press fifteen, or eighteen" and he twisted for a look at her. "Still doing that?" he said.

"I'll stop when she's twenty. I think that'll just make me feel old."

He hesitated before entering the code, glancing around for his shorts. He didn't want to talk to his daughter standing naked and foolish in the hotel room. But in the next moment the phone was sounding in his hand. He read the luminous little window. "It's Shawn."

"Good boy," she said.

He lifted the phone to his ear. "Hello, Shawn."

Hey, Dad, he heard in his mind, in expectation—the first two words he ever heard out of his son on the phone. Heard them so clearly that when he heard something else, in someone else's voice, his head jerked as if struck.

"Is this Mr. Courtland?" a man asked.

"Yes. Who is this?"

At these words, the change in his body, Angela came around to look at his face. He met her eyes briefly then looked away, out the window again. The man on the phone identified himself in some detail, but all Grant caught was the word *sheriff*.

"What's happened?" he asked. "Where's Shawn?" There was a pain in his forearm and he looked down to see Angela's fingers clamped there, the nails embedded. He pried at them gently.

"He's here at the Medical Center in Granby, Mr. Courtland," said the sheriff. "He's a tad banged up but the doc says he'll be fine. I found his wallet and this phone in his—"

"What do you mean a tad—" He stopped himself. "What do you mean by that?"

"I mean it looks like he got himself in some kind of accident up there on the mountain, Mr. Courtland. I ain't had a chance to talk to him yet, they doped him pretty quick for the . . . well, you can talk to the doc in a second here. But first—"

"But he's all right," Grant said.

"Oh, his leg's busted pretty good. But he was wearing that helmet. He'll be just fine. He had some good luck up there."

"What do you mean?"

"I mean he could've laid there a lot longer, where he was, but it happened some folks come by on their bikes. Nice young couple."

Grant's heart thudded up in his skull. He couldn't think, his mind too full of the boy lying there, up there—

"Mr. Courtland," said the sheriff. "Where are you all at?"

There was something in the man's tone. Grant shook his head. "What do you mean?"

"Well, sir. We found your boy way up there on the mountain, on a rented bike. So I'm wondering where *you're* at."

"Caitlin," Angela suddenly said, her eyes fierce—and Grant's heart leapt and he said, "Yes. Let me speak to my daughter. Let me speak to Caitlin."

"Your daughter—?" said the other man, and was silent. In the silence was the sound of his breathing; was the sound of him making an adjustment to his sheriff's belt; a woman's voice paging unintelligibly down the empty hospital corridor. When the sheriff spoke again he sounded like a different man altogether.

"Mr. Courtland," he said, and with his skidding heart Grant stepped toward the window, as if he would walk right through it, into the mountains—the green hills so close, humped one upon the other like a heaving sea. Angela stopped him physically, her thumbs in his biceps. She stood so close she could hear every sound from the tiny speaker. "Mr. Courtland," said the sheriff. "Your son came in alone."

"No," she said. Shaking her head. Beneath her thumbs his arteries swelled and beat. *"No,"* she said, and turned away, and went to the suitcases near the bathroom.

For her, Grant knew, it was simple: there was a God, but He was a God for whom no cruelty was unthinkable, and against whom the only defense was the human heart—the love and the fierceness that He Himself had put into it, into hers. She would not allow this to happen to her, not again. Already she was getting dressed. Already she had a plan.

When they were young, when they were naked and young in that apartment of hers above the bakery, he tracked her heartbeat by the little cross she wore—the slightest, most delicate movements down in that hollow, that tender pit of throat. He touched the cross with his finger and asked without thinking, Wasn't it ironic, though?

Wasn't what?

That God took your twin sister, whose name was Faith?

She turned away. She wept, and he said, I'm sorry . . . please, Angela, I'm sorry . . . He didn't yet know of the other heart, the tiniest heart, beating with hers.

And now, in the awful little hotel room, with the phone still to his ear, Grant was begging again. Begging for forgiveness, pleading, and making such desperate promises as he'd never made in his life . . . *Dear God, Dear God* . . . and all the while the sheriff was asking him again where he was at, telling him to stay put. The boy was safe, he was asleep. He was coming to get them, the sheriff, no more than thirty minutes. He would take them up there himself, up the mountain. He would take them wherever they needed to go. But they wouldn't be there when the sheriff arrived, Grant knew. They would already be on the mountain, on their way up. The boy was safe. The boy was asleep. Grant would be at the wheel and Angela would be at the maps, the way it was in the life before, the way it would be in the life to come.

Irish Girl

The way it began, the way he'd remember it many years later, was a kick to the leg.

He was under the kitchen table playing with army men and somebody kicked him. Not too hard but not too soft, either.

William.

He turned and scowled at corduroys and tube socks, all he could see of his brother. "What?"

"They're waiting for you," William said in an odd voice. "In their bedroom."

And then he walked away.

Before that, of course, were things Charlie didn't know much about, being eight. He didn't know about Nixon's decision to send troops into Cambodia, or how that led to the shootings at Kent State, or how that led, in turn, to the smashed shop windows in his own home town. He did know a little about the thirteen boys from the agricultural college arrested for rioting, because his father had been their lawyer. But he didn't know how the trial, which had made the news every night for two weeks, spreading his father's name across the state like goldenrod, had given his father the idea to run for office. He didn't know what the Iowa House of Representatives was, or what people did with all those leaflets he left on their porches, or what it meant to win by a landslide. And he didn't know his father was still riding the high of victory when he decided, a few days before leaving for the State Capitol, to have The Talk.

He didn't know that's where William had just come from, he only knew he'd been under the kitchen table, playing with army men, when his brother kicked him.

⸫

It was true: his parents were waiting for him, sitting on the edge of their bed and beaming at him with wet eyes. His father sat him down and explained what adopted meant even though Charlie already knew from school; when you picked on the adopted kid he'd fight and say it was a lie, as if being adopted was the worst thing ever, worse than having no dad at all. Charlie stared at the floor and felt sick to his stomach, waiting for his parents to tell him he was adopted, too. Finally, he had to ask.

His father leaned forward. He was a big man to begin with and when he leaned forward you couldn't see anything else, he was it. "Would you be sad if you were?" his father asked.

Charlie knew what his father wanted to hear—that Charlie wouldn't give a dog's fart because he still had the best parents in the world, who would love him forever.

But all he could do was shrug.

"Well," his father said at last. "You're not adopted, Charlie. You came from your mom and me." He put his hands on Charlie's shoulders. "But that doesn't mean we love you any more or any less than William, or that he's not your real brother. You understand? You boys will be brothers forever."

Charlie understood, but he was so happy not to be adopted he wanted to spread the news, he wanted to put it on a leaflet and hit every porch in the world.

That night, Charlie sat down to dinner like a kid moving underwater, trying to look normal. William was still in the room the boys shared, no light showing under the door. A January wind was in the seams of the back door, moaning eerily. The house, the whole neighborhood, kept its back to open farmland and bore the first, hardest blows of weather. In the spring the air was soaked in the smell of soil and manure, and at night you heard the cows bawl, and the horn of the freight trains was to warn them, William said, to stay off the tracks or else.

Charlie pushed beans around on his plate and hated himself for being glad he wasn't adopted. He told himself that if anyone ever teased the adopted kid at school again he'd help him fight, he swore to God he would.

"Hey, baby," his mother said, and his father lowered his cup of coffee.

Charlie turned and there was William. Hands in his pockets, squinting in the light. He stared at them, and for a second it looked like he might turn and leave, and that's when Charlie moved. Jumped up and ran to him, locked his arms around him so tightly it was hard for William to get his hands out of his pockets. Finally he did, wiggled them out from under Charlie's grip, and got his fingers around Charlie's biceps and moved him, just so, aside. "Lay off, willya?" he said. "I'm hungry."

And that was that. The boys sat down, and Charlie didn't whimper or even rub at the matching dents of pain in his arms where William had sunk his thumbs to the bone.

———

Their father bought a second car for his trips to Des Moines, a green Cougar convertible, and one Sunday early in his term he took William and Charlie with him to show them where he sat in the session chamber, and they spent the night with him in the cramped, untidy trailer he rented near the interstate.

"You think he likes this place more than home?" Charlie asked William that night. Their father had gone to meet someone, and William had his legs stretched out on a nappy brown sofa, studying the pages of a *PLAYBOY* he'd found under the cushions. The trailer smelled like the inside of leather shoes and shower mildew and old pizza boxes, and Charlie could feel the hum of tractor-trailers through a stiff layer of carpet.

"Shit, Charlie," his brother replied, rising and heading for the toilet. "Wouldn't you?"

Their father brought them home, and the next morning returned to Des Moines, and then didn't come home again for months, and this was because he was writing bills and had to work extra hard to get them made into laws, Charlie's mother said. William just stared at her, the same look on his face that always let Charlie know he'd said something really stupid, then walked away. He'd stopped cutting his hair and had begun to smell like cigarettes and car engines. At night when he came in, he'd crash into his bed with superhero exhaustion, as if he'd been pushed to the very limit of his powers. In the mornings Charlie watched him plod across the room in his underwear, his boner out before him like the nose of a German shepherd, and felt so puny he wanted to scream. He checked himself daily for signs of growth, but nothing changed, and he worried that something was wrong with him and that when William was a full-grown man, he would still be the hairless little nothing he was right then.

William was right about their father preferring a smelly trailer to home, because when his two-year term was over and he went back to his law practice, he moved into another one in their hometown. He picked the boys up on Fridays in the Cougar and the three of them ate pizza and went out for breakfast and saw matinees and sat around the trailer watching TV until Sunday afternoon, when their father would let William, who by now had a driver's permit, drive them back to the house.

During the week, when Charlie got home from school he'd find William and his friends strewn in front of the TV like dead men, drinking Cokes and licking potato chip grease from their fingers. The boys called William Billy, and Charlie knew they had all cut school early, if they'd gone at all. William made sure to clear them out by the time their mother got home, but she could count Cokes and read the air with her nose, and she and William would both start yelling and Charlie would shut himself in his room until he heard the front door slam and he knew William had gone out again.

One night, when she tried to keep William home for dinner, he told her to get off his back and she slapped him. Her handprint spread like a warning light over his face, and for a second Charlie thought he was going to slap her back. "Bitch," he said, and she took a step back like he'd gone ahead and done it. Then he left, and the word "adopted" rose in Charlie's throat like vomit, and he wanted to remind her that's what William was and why he'd said it, because no real son, no flesh-and-blood son, would ever call his mother that name.

Later that night, Charlie got up to pee and heard her on the phone. She said "Mason," their father's name, with a wobble in her throat, and when he came to get the boys the following Friday, for their weekend, William brought along two pillow cases full of clothes.

⁛

Charlie didn't miss William until the spring, when he began to hear the cows at night and the moaning trains and he'd remember how he used to sit on William's bed with a flashlight while William made up stories about a gang of killers, whacked-out hippies forever hopping off trains and shooting people. Somehow the hippies always made their way across the fields right up to the living room window where Mason and Connie Whitford sat watching the news of the killing spree. When he told his stories, William's eyes grew brilliant, super-blue, and they lit up a place where he and Charlie were equals, where they snapped into action at the exact same moment and they never failed.

That April, after a month with William, Mason gave up trailers for good. He bought a house, a big old one in the middle of town, and when Charlie arrived for his first weekend he was amazed to learn that the upstairs bedroom with the new bed and the matching dresser and desk and the three windows was all for him. William had his own room on the other side of the wall and Mason's was at the far end of the hall and had its own bathroom. Downstairs, you could reach full speed running from one end of the house to the other, and below that was a basement with a pool table the previous owner had left behind.

His first night in the new house Charlie lay awake for hours, getting used to the shadows of the room and the drone of traffic outside his window. He was finally drifting off when the horn of a freight train, a single short blast, punched through and jerked him back. Warning bells rang in the streets and the horn sounded again, louder this time, so loud he was sure the train was heading right for the house. But the next blast of the horn was weaker, a deflating balloon, and he heard the clacking of the wheels on the rails and it calmed his heart, that rhythm, and he slept.

Mason came downstairs the next night stinking of Brut after-shave and wearing blue jeans that made Charlie laugh. He was going out to dinner with a friend, he told them, and William was in charge.

William stared at the TV. The Six-Million-Dollar Man was jumping a wall.

"William," his father said.

"Yeah?"

"I said you're going to be in charge for a few hours. Can you handle that?"

"No sweat."

Charlie watched his father standing there squeezing his car keys in his fist, his eyes dark, and for the first time in his life Charlie actually wanted him to go, to leave them alone.

Finally, with a pat to Charlie's head, he did.

"Who's his friend?" Charlie asked when their father was gone.

"What day of the week is it?"

Charlie told him but William just smirked and lit a Camel.

"Dad lets you smoke?"

"Fuck, no." He got up and moved to the open window. "Dad's a fascist."

"What's that?"

"He's the guy who ends up full of bullet holes with old ladies pissing on him in the town square."

Charlie chewed an already raw fingernail. He couldn't believe the things a sixteen-year-old knew, especially one who never went to school.

William eyed him. "You gonna narc on me?"

Charlie shook his head and William took a studious drag on the cigarette. "How 'bout if I split for a while? You gonna be cool with that?"

"If you take me with you."

"Not a chance."

A car horn honked loudly, once, and William flicked his cigarette out the window. Charlie jumped up, but William put a hand on his shoulder, sunk his thumb into the flesh above his collar bone. "I can count on you, Charlie, can't I?" The pressure made Charlie feel like a puppet, like William could make his legs buckle with just the right kind of squeeze.

"Yes," he said, refusing to squirm.

"Promise to God and hope to die?"

"Yes."

William let go. "Outstanding," he said, and then he left, banging the screen door behind him. Charlie watched him climb behind the wheel of a Chevy Impala the color of an army tank. A girl with straight red hair mashed her lips against his for a full minute, her fingers deep in his hair, before he finally gunned the engine and backed out of the drive, leaving tracks.

Two hours later Mason called, and Charlie picked up.

———

Something was coming down the hallway, fast and loud in the middle of the night.

His bed shook and wood exploded and Charlie flattened himself against the mattress, ready for the floor to drop out from under him. "Get up!" his father yelled.

Not at Charlie. At William, on the other side of the wall. He was in William's room. He'd kicked in the door.

"What for?" William tried to sound tough.

"Because I told you to."

"Christ, Dad. Can't it—"

Bedsprings creaked and something hit the floor, and Charlie heard footsteps like two giant kids practicing a dance. "Get! Up!" Mason yelled. "Get up when I tell you!" The dance thudded out into the hall and something, an elbow or a head, bounced against Charlie's door. "Open the door when I tell you," his father said. "Watch your brother when I tell you."

"He can watch himself! He's not a baby!"

"I don't care."

They moved down the hall, and Charlie heard William grunt and his father bark back, "Don't you—don't you even try it," and Charlie's bed picked up the shock waves of William slamming into a wall. "Whattaya gonna do, *Dad?*" William's voice rose and came apart. "Gonna hit me? Go ahead! Hit me! Hit me, *Dad!*"

"Don't test me, William, I warn you."

And then the dance moved on, in bursts and thuds, down the stairs and all the way to the opposite end of the house, where it either stopped or merely ceased to distinguish itself, at that distance, from Charlie's banging heart.

———

In the morning, Charlie made an inspection of the door. The jamb was split vertically, and a shard of it lay in the middle of William's room, the brass strike plate still attached and looking stunned, like a mouth knocked from a face.

Charlie spent the rest of the day pretending to read comic books or watch TV, waiting to see William. But he never showed up, and Charlie went back to his mother's thinking William had stayed away because of him—that he never wanted to see Charlie's ugly little narc face again.

He didn't see William again until the following Saturday afternoon. Mason was in the middle of a trial and had gone to the office, so Charlie was alone in the house when William walked in and slugged him in the shoulder. Charlie raised his arms, expecting more, but William was grinning.

"Get your shoes, Charlie Horse."

Outside, Charlie saw the tank-colored Chevy and stopped short. Blood filled his chest. He couldn't breathe right.

"What's with you?" William worked up a gob of spit, sent it flying. "Look," he said. "I promise you'll be back before he ever knows you were gone. OK?"

The car was full of big teenagers with long hair and army jackets like William's—and the girl Charlie had seen before with the straight red hair. She and one of the boys shifted to let William behind the wheel, and two boys in back made room for Charlie. "Fuckin' A!" a boy with great shining pimples said. "Fresh troops!" He blew smoke in Charlie's face that didn't smell like cigarettes.

Charlie coughed, and the girl craned around and stunned him with white teeth and the biggest, greenest eyes he'd ever seen. She looked right at him and kept smiling and said, "Happy Birthday, Charlie."

The girl's name was Colleen and she was a Foosball wizard. Three times during the game she held the ball in place with one of her men while she put her hand over Charlie's and moved his men just so. Then, with a snap of her wrist he couldn't even see, she scored on William and the boy with pimples. William laughed, but the boy with pimples called her a cheater and she told him to grow up, dickweed. The boy glared at Charlie and asked William, out of the side of his mouth as if Charlie wouldn't hear him that way, "He retarded, or what?"

William stared hard at the boy, then gave Charlie a grin. "You retarded, Charlie?"

Charlie was still floating from Colleen's hand on his, and he couldn't imagine any idiot thing a dickweed with pimples could say to bring him down, so he just shook his head.

"He don't say much, do he," the boy said, and William said, "No he don't. But he's thinking, man. He thinks more in a day than you do in a year."

"Right," the boy said, and Colleen snapped her wrist and the ball disappeared with a bang.

When it was time to go, William had to drag Charlie from the pinball machines, but Charlie was twelve, too old to make a scene, so he jammed his hands in his pockets and tried to look bored. William hooked an arm around Colleen and dropped his hand on her breast for a quick, secret squeeze. "Back in a flash," he told her. She smiled at Charlie and it was too much, he had to look away.

William drove fast, a grim expression on his face, and when they came to the railroad tracks he locked up the brakes and pounded the steering wheel so hard Charlie couldn't believe it didn't crack. They were at the end of a line of cars waiting for a train to pass. The central hub of the Rock Island Railway was not far away, and the people who lived here, it sometimes seemed, lived in the spaces between its lines like prisoners. Freighters plowed through day and night, trains without head or tail, and there was nothing you could do but sit and wait.

William jammed the Chevy into park and thumbed in the electric lighter. He pushed his hair back from his face, lit a Camel, and dropped the pack on the seat. Charlie breathed in the first cloud of smoke, always the best-smelling one, and picked up the pack. William didn't seem to notice or care as Charlie pulled out one of the Camels with his lips, the way William did. And he didn't budge when Charlie pushed in the electric lighter. But when the lighter popped and Charlie steered the red coil toward the tip of the Camel, his brother reached over and plucked the cigarette from his mouth.

"You gotta do everything I do? You want Mason breaking down your door at 2 a.m.?"

Charlie recalled that night and was disgusted with himself—cowering in his room like a pussy while William got the crap beaten out of him, all because Charlie hadn't been smart enough, or brave enough, to come up with a lie on the phone.

He'd tell him he was sorry, he decided. Right now.

He'd tell him before that red boxcar crossed the road . . .

Before the end of the train . . .

But he didn't, and he didn't, and the red lights stopped flashing and the Chevy was moving again and Charlie watched his chance slip away with the caboose.

William whipped into the driveway and braked at the last second, just shy of Mason's Cougar. He shifted into Reverse and tossed Charlie a salute. "Happy Birthday, man."

"You're not coming in?"

"Naw. I gotta go get those losers."

Charlie gripped his left hand in his right, remembering the Foosball game. His heart would not slow down.

"I like the girl," he said.

"Colleen?"

He turned and William smiled and Charlie saw a light in his eyes he hadn't seen in so long he'd forgotten it even existed.

"You know what her name means?" William asked.

It was the light, Charlie realized, from the nights when they shared a room and William told stories and they had no idea that one of them was adopted.

"What's it mean?" he asked.

William took a deep drag on the cigarette and stared out the windshield. "Means, *Irish girl.*"

—◦◦◦—

Mason was in the kitchen, leaning against the counter with his hands in his pockets, jingling change and keys. "Where'd he take you?" he said quietly.

Charlie glanced into the dining room and saw a chocolate bakery cake with unlit candles and a small pile of gifts on the table. "Nowhere."

"Nowhere?"

He shrugged and felt a wet heat in his armpits, a weakness in his legs that told him what a terrible thing he was about to do. But he did it anyway, and for no good reason except that he hadn't been able to do it the night he should've.

"We went to the movies," he lied. "It was my birthday present." He took a step toward the stairs, but Mason grabbed his arm, pulled him back into the kitchen.

"Don't you walk away from me."

"Let me go!" Charlie wasn't afraid, exactly, his father had never hit him his whole life, but he wanted out of that grip before the tears came and ruined everything.

"You reek of smoke, Charlie. You reek of smoke and pot. Were you smoking pot in that car?"

"What?"

"Did you smoke anything with William?"

"No!"

"Don't you lie to me."

"I'm not!"

Mason had a hold of both arms now, squeezing to the bone, and he was shaking him, a low, rapid jerking that seemed beyond his control. Charlie watched his father's face redden and saw the look in his eyes and thought he was maybe having a heart attack. "Dad," he said. "Dad!" He grabbed his father's wrists and squeezed but his father just held on, staring at him so intensely, so strangely, that Charlie would wonder later if it wasn't at that exact second that William tried to beat the train.

For this to be true he'd have to have driven very fast after dropping Charlie off, in a rush to get back to his friends, back to Colleen. Or maybe the blue light was in his eyes and he drove the only way he knew how when he felt like that, like a man from another planet, like a superhero. Charlie sees him flicking his Camel out the window and gripping the wheel in both hands. He sees his boot stomp the gas pedal and the muscles of his jaw grow hard as the Chevy leaps, and he sees his eyes, the light, the flash of blue wonder, the moment he knows he's not going to make it.

Everything after that seems to happen through a cracked window, with Charlie standing outside looking in. There's the police in the house, led there by a driver's license. There's the drive across town and the sound Charlie can hear, sitting in the Cougar in the driveway, of his mother at the kitchen table, her cry a piercing thing, a teapot beginning to boil, a January wind. There's the funeral and William's friends in their cheap ties and army jackets sulking like war buddies. And there's Colleen, wrapping her arms around Charlie so fiercely, so hungrily that he knows she doesn't know—that she believes Charlie is a true brother, a living blood link to the body in the coffin.

And after that there's just the long withering summer, the weekends with his father, the two of them going out for meals, going to movies, taking long drives at night with the top down. One Saturday a carpenter comes, an old guy who gets Charlie to help him carry his tools up the stairs and hand him the things he asks for, and when they're done, William's door looks good as new, the brass strike plate, that shocked little mouth, back in place. At the end of the summer the house is sold and Charlie moves in with Mason for the school year, into a two-bedroom house close to Charlie's new school, and they begin to eat at home in the evenings and Mason begins a new trial and Charlie learns that a pretty girl at school likes him—and still.

Still it's the same town, and when they go somewhere in the Cougar, no matter what streets they take or how they time it, they end up stuck before a passing train. When this happens they don't talk and they don't look at each other, though Charlie would like to know what his father is thinking, if he's thinking about the night he kicked down William's door, or something better, like teaching him to ride a bike, or maybe the day they brought him home, their new son. If his father asked him, Charlie would try to describe the last time he saw William—the look in his eyes, the blue light, the wild secret rush when William said the words *Irish girl*.

But his father doesn't ask and the train is a long one, and so they sit there, having no choice, and watch for its end.

LaVergne, TN USA
09 March 2010
175339LV00002B/1/P